Anna
AND THE *King*

SECTION
58

ALSO AVAILABLE FROM
HARPERENTERTAINMENT

The Story of Anna and the King
by Cecelia Holland

Anna AND THE King

NOVELIZATION BY
ELIZABETH HAND

Based on the screenplay by
Steve Meerson & Peter Krikes
and Andy Tennant & Rick Parks

HarperEntertainment
An Imprint of HarperCollinsPublishers

🏰 HarperEntertainment

An Imprintof HarperCollins*Publishers*

10 East 53rd Street, New York, NY 10022–5299

ISBN 0-06-102045-1

HarperCollins®, 🏰®, and HarperEntertainment™
are trademarks of HarperCollins Publishers Inc.

First Printing: December 1999

Printed in the United States of America

Visit HarperEntertainment on the World Wide Web at
www.harpercollins.com

99 00 01 02 03 🏰 10 9 8 7 6 5 4 3 2 1

B 25437

one

*S*he was the first Englishwoman I had ever
met. And it seemed to me she knew more
about the world than anyone.

For weeks the monsoon winds had whispered her
arrival like a coming storm, until it seemed that her
name echoed within our dreams, insistent as wind
and thunder. Some welcomed the coming rain, while
others feared a raging flood. Still she came, and like
the autumn rains, there was no stopping her once she
was in our midst.

Please understand, I was only a child then. Twelve,
the same age my father had been when his father put
him in charge of our country's military forces, its regi-
ments of horse and elephant, the ranks of bowmen and
foot soldiers in their gold and crimson livery. But I am

1

not my father, and whatever face I turned to the world in those heady days, secretly I felt myself still to be a child, albeit the son of a king. And so it was that, like our teacher, I was unaware of the suspicion that preceded her arrival within the sacred enclave of our court, in the months after she responded to my father's letter.

And it was not until years later that I began to appreciate how brave she was. And how alone she must have felt.

An Englishwoman . . . the first I'd ever met . . .

English Era, 1862, 26th February

Grand Royal Palace, Bangkok

To Mrs. A. H. Leonowens:

Madam: We are in good pleasure, and satisfaction in heart, that you are in willingness to undertake the education of our beloved royal children. And we hope that in doing your education on us and on our children (whom English call inhabitants of benighted land), you will do your best endeavor for knowledge of English language, science, and literature, and not for conversion to Christianity; as the followers of Buddha are mostly aware of the power-

2

fulness of truth and virtue, as well as the followers of Christ, and are desirous to have facility of English language and literature more than new religions.

We beg to invite you to our royal palace to do your best endeavorment upon us and our children. We shall expect to see you here on return of Siamese steamer *Chow Pya*.

We have written to Mr. William Anderson, and to our consul at Singapore, to authorize to do best arrangement for you and ourselves.

Believe me
Your faithfully,
(Signed) S.S.P.P. Maha Mongkut
His Majesty Phra Chom Klao, Rama IV

Bombay had been a daydream—heat and color, the sickly sweet odor of fenugreek, spilled turmeric staining her fingers yellow, and the sun like a crushed blossom blooming overhead. And like a daydream her sojourn there had been too short, cradled within the larger, safer dream of a long afternoon in the city's British colony, fragrant with bergamot-scented tea and the raisin-studded scones which Anna herself baked, because her husband loved them.

Bangkok was no daydream. Indeed, as she sat

3

within her stateroom on the steamer *Newcastle*, she could scarcely imagine sleeping here at all. From outside the little oval window echoed a din of voices—the cries of boatmen angling their narrow-prowed canoes through the harbor, the shouts of men and women onshore, and the shrill accusations of gulls and more exotic birds sweeping above them all. A thousand shrieking, laughing, singing, bartering, bantering voices, rising and falling in the bright cadences of every language of the East: Chinese, Malaysian, the dialects of Khmer and Laos and Java.

And, of course, Siamese.

Thoughtfully, and for the hundredth time, Anna smoothed the voluminous folds of her silken dress, then picked up the letter on the bed beside her, its envelope bearing the crimson seal of the Royal Court of Siam. She opened it and carefully unfolded the page inside. Black ink on thick cream-colored paper, the English letters carefully formed.

To Mrs. A. H. Leonowens:

Madam: We are in good pleasure, and satisfaction in heart, that you are in willingness to undertake the education of our beloved royal children . . .

4

• • •

She reread it, frowning slightly, then ran her finger over the page, trying to divine something from the words besides their formal invitation. And indeed she almost felt that she could sense him there, in the swirls and heavily inked capitals, the tiny holes left where the quill pen had stabbed the page, punctuating the end of each sentence as though pronouncing judgment upon the reader.

"Mrs. Leonowens?"

A sharp rap at the door of her stateroom. Anna looked up, biting her lip; she quickly folded the letter and replaced it in the envelope. She stood, running her hands across her hair in its neat coif and then resting her palms upon her cheeks. Hot, and there were tears at the corner of her eyes, the only outward signs of her fear—oh, say it!—her *terror* at being alone in this place, a thousand miles from anyplace she had ever called home, and with no one to blame but herself—and, perhaps, the man who had written the letter on her bed.

She closed her eyes, seeking the peace and resolve that Moonshee had taught her could be summoned in this manner, and took a deep breath. "Come in," she said in a low, calm voice.

The door opened. Captain Orton stood there, a young steward at his side.

"Mrs. Leonowens, I'm afraid the tide won't wait. Not even for you," he added with a gallant smile.

Anna forced a smile in return. "Thank you, Captain. You have been more than patient with me."

"I really shouldn't allow you to disembark without an escort—"

The captain gestured at the door, and Anna swept out, skirts rustling. "Nonsense," she said, tilting her chin and giving him a flash of her blue-gray eyes. "You should know better, Captain—I'm not one of your wilting English roses! I've spent years in India—"

The captain shook his head and peered after her into the dim, narrow corridor belowdecks. "This isn't Bombay, madam, or even Singapore, for that matter. It is rather more . . . *primitive* . . . out there."

"Which is precisely why I'm here," retorted Anna with rather more confidence than she felt. But as she mounted the ladder to the upper deck, she caught a glimpse of Captain Orton's admiring glance, and knew—for the moment, at least—that she'd convinced him.

If only I could convince myself, she thought ruefully. But before her resolve could falter, she was on deck, assaulted by sunlight and that cacophony of voices. And one of them belonged to Louis, her ten-year-old son. He stood at the rail, perched on a coil of rope and watching a group of dock workers struggling with a clumsy block-and-tackle apparatus. They were attempting to lift a pallet laden with cartons and luggage and baskets of livestock, when suddenly the rope snapped. The workers ran, shouting, as the pallet crashed to the ground, its contents scattering everywhere.

"Mother!" Louis pointed excitedly. "Mother, come look! I think they've killed someone!"

Anna hurried over, staring down at where hundreds of people continued about their business, unperturbed by the accident. If they *had* killed someone, no one seemed to have noticed. "Careful by the rail, darling." He gave her a quick smile and she melted, seeing in his deep blue eyes the very image of his father, her late husband. "Where are Beebe and Moonshee?"

Louis turned and pointed to where an Indian woman in her fifties struggled with a heavy valise. "There's Beebe—"

"Beebe! Moonshee," called Anna. "Gather your things. It's time we went to shore."

Panting heavily, the small imperious Indian woman bustled across the deck, tugging the folds of her orange sari when they threatened to catch upon a bamboo birdcage. Behind her a bearded man scowled at a passing porter.

"You, sir!" he cried, and snatched a small portrait of Queen Victoria from the bemused porter's hands. "I will thank you to show *respect*."

Another porter staggered past, carrying the crate containing Anna's good china. "Those are family heirlooms!" she shouted. "Please try to be careful—"

Beebe hurried up alongside Anna, pausing momentarily to grab a huge valise from a pile of luggage. "What sort of culture allows a proper woman to fend for herself in such a godforsaken place?"

"I agree utterly, Beebe," her husband replied. He looked sternly at Anna. "I still think we should wait until someone from the palace arrives."

Anna shook her head. "No. If they were coming, Moonshee, they would've been here already. Besides, the ship is leaving—"

"My point exactly!" cried Moonshee.

Anna ignored him. In one hand she clutched her

8

Siamese primer, a gift from the Siamese consul at Singapore, the last posting her husband had held before his death. Her other hand tightened around her son's, and she pulled him close to her. She turned, gazing across the *Newcastle*'s deck to where the Chao Phraya River flowed, a veritable highway crowded with clipper ships and schooners, canoes and Chinese junks. Dozens of flags fluttered above the vessels, from as many nations; and over all of them, like a watchful giant, loomed the vast ramparts and spires of Fort Paknam.

"Look," she murmured, gazing down upon the dock. Workers struggled with a guyline attached to a pallet laden with crates and bags—their own. "It's time now—it's time—"

And with Louis and Moonshee and Beebe in tow, she turned and strode down the gangplank, leaving one strange world for a newer, stranger one. Louis clutched his cricket bat as though it might protect him. Anna looked around distractedly, trying to make sense of the surrounding chaos. Captain Orton had said this was the customs house, but if so it was unlike any official port of entry she had ever seen—a massive outdoor market, crowded with men and women and animals, and all of them seemingly intent upon separating Anna Leonowens from her little entourage.

For an instant it seemed they had succeeded: when Anna looked down, Louis was gone. She whirled in a panic, then saw him over by the broken pallet, listening to the bickering workers. "*Louis—*"

She grabbed him and pulled him away. He craned his neck, still straining to watch, and asked, "Mother, why does this king need you if nobody here speaks English?"

"Because, sweetheart, the ways of England are the ways of the world. It's a wise man who knows that."

They struggled to make their way through a fish market, dodging nets of squid and octopus and prawns, along with numerous creatures Anna had never seen before and a few she wished she'd never glimpsed. Ahead of them a wave of people holding official papers fought their way to a desk where a beleaguered man sat, frowning. The wave crested and broke around him—interpreters, government inspectors, businessmen, all haggling and pointing furiously at the pallets of imported goods heaped upon the dock. As Anna and her family approached, first one and then another of the eager merchants fixed them with a suspicious glare, occasionally sharpening into downright hostility. Moonshee glared back, then turned to Anna.

"Memsahib, in less than an hour the *Newscastle* sails, not to return for a month."

"Tonight we shall all sleep in our own beds in our own home, I promise," said Anna. A toothless old woman passed them, and Anna reached out to tentatively pluck her arm. "Pardon us, please—where would we find a carriage?"

The woman stared at her blankly. Anna flipped through her primer, then asked in halting Siamese, "A carriage?"

The woman nodded, then pointed at a massive pair of gates. Anna smiled and beckoned her little family to follow her.

Louis brandished his cricket bat like a sword. "Don't worry, Mother—I'll protect you!"

"Thank you, dear—" Her eyes widened. "Louis! Mind the crocodile!" Pulling up her skirts, Anna sidestepped a black-clad merchant leading an enormous lizard on a woven tether.

"Yeow!" cried Louis, while Moonshee eyed the creature measuringly.

"Monitor lizard," he pronounced. "I have not seen one since I was a child."

11

"I would be happy not seeing one now," said Beebe.

"Mother!" Louis craned his neck as the merchant led his prize away. "Is that a *pet*? Can I have one? Please!"

Moonshee shook his head. "Ah! Stay close, little brother, or that creature will not be the only thing on a leash."

Louis nodded sadly as the lizard disappeared into the crowd, and they continued on through the market. Anna tried not to look confused, or frightened, or worried, but it was harder not to look amazed by all the intensely strange things around them. Vendors carried bushels of unrecognizable fruits and vegetables; rainbow-colored birds in bamboo cages; baskets of stag beetles, the insects the size of a small child's hand. Anna slid her arm around Louis's shoulder and pulled him protectively to her side, as much for her own comfort as his.

"What do you suppose he's like?" she said. "This King Mongkut?" Louis shrugged, too intent on the market to answer. "I've heard that commoners used to be forbidden to even look upon King Mongkut's face. The Siamese consul back in Singapore told me that they revere him as a god."

12

"Like Jesus?" asked Louis.

"Hardly," sniffed Anna. "But if he wishes for his son the crown prince to be tutored in the ways of the West—well, I suppose I should be quite honored."

"Why can't he just send him to London?"

"Because then *you* wouldn't have the chance to learn Siamese."

They found a hackney carriage, and through a combination of sign language and bits of phrases from her primer, Anna arranged for them to be taken to the palace. A carriage was not the most ordinary mode of transport, in a city where even rickshaws had not yet made an appearance, and where the number of people thronging the narrow streets seemed as limitless as the schools of bright fish Anna glimpsed in the river. But then, Anna and her entourage were not quite ordinary visitors.

"I miss Bombay," said Louis dejectedly. In his lap was his father's uniform hat, its wilted plume a mournful symbol of how they all felt.

"I know," whispered Anna. She wrapped her arms around her son. "So do I . . ."

Outside the carriage bobbed rows of floating houses, built upon the banks of the *klongs*—canals—and anchored to heavy posts. Their roofs

13

were of woven thatch, and many of them looked so flimsy that Anna marveled that the heavy monsoon winds had not blown them away. But the *klongs* at least had an illusion of serenity—blue water reflecting bluer sky, narrow-prowed canoes and sampans darting across the surface like water striders.

The streets in comparison were a noisy, steaming place, the muddy ground churned up by carriages and thousands of bare feet. Everywhere was the smell of rotting fish, the sweetish scent of the banana leaves used for steaming rice. The road was stained red with betel juice. Waxen clusters of frangipani blossoms overhung the street, and there were clusters of mango trees thick with heavenly fruit—an irresistible sight to Louis, who early toppled from the cab as he tried to grab one.

"Be more careful, little brother," scolded Moonshee as he caught the boy's waist. "We would never find you *there* if you fell!"

At the word "there" he jabbed his finger, indicating the crowd outside the little carriage window. Louis looked and nodded soberly. A jostling mass of people hurried past them along the canal bank, and now and then the cry *Farang! Farang!* would break out as someone caught a glimpse of the light-skinned Westerners peering from the carriage.

"You see now what it is like to be different," Anna said in a low voice to her son. Their time in Bombay had made her acutely aware of the terrible injustices brought upon those whose skin color, or rank, or caste set them apart from others. The protected hothouse atmosphere of the British colony there had occasionally been oppressive, and when a missionary friend had given Anna a copy of an inflammatory novel by the American author Harriet Beecher Stowe, Anna had devoured it, later reading it aloud to not just Louis but Beebe and Moonshee as well. As the hansom rounded a corner, a small group of young men jumped up from their seats outside a floating house and raced along the narrow path after the coach, pointing at Anna and Louis excitedly. "It's a strange feeling, isn't it?"

"Mother! *Look!*" Once again Louis practically leaped through the cab's window, but this time even Moonshee appeared startled. "Mother! *Elephants!*"

"Goodness!" Anna gasped and covered her mouth with her hand. Above them loomed a column of elephants in full military regalia, all seemingly oblivious to the carriage as they shambled past it in single file.

"Gracious me!" cried Beebe. "Are we sure this is the right road?"

Louis pushed his mother's restraining arms aside and leaned out the window again. Beside him Moonshee tilted his head, trying to peer around the vast moving wall of gray flesh and golden caparisons.

"How would we know?" he said with a droll wink at the boy. "If you are not the lead elephant, the scenery never changes."

The carriage jounced along, its passengers vying with each other to catch a glimpse of the Secret City outside the hansom's windows. Minutes later, they were outside the palace gates.

"*Oh.*" Anna's voice was scarcely above a whisper. Beside her, Louis and Moonshee and Beebe were silent. "Oh, my . . ."

Nothing on earth could have prepared her for it. An entire royal compound that was a city unto itself, but to Western eyes, more a rapturous, lapidary dream of a city than anything Anna could have imagined. Throne halls and temples, pavilions and gilded columns, arched gateways and carven gables—an endless vista of glittering buildings, extending more than twenty city blocks, as far as the eye could see.

Spires and pillars reached skyward, buttressed with life-size elephants carved in marble. Immense roofs shaped like golden bells, and tiered spires, and serrated upper stories flanking Bodhi trees of gold and crimson and emerald green. And everywhere the images of a thousand wondrous creatures: *nagas* and *kinnarees*, bird-women and sacred snakes; glaring temple guardians three stories tall, their bodies encrusted with precious stones; wooden temple dancers and gilded lions, bronze effigies and the omnipresent Garuda, Vishnu's sacred steed: a warrior with an eagle's beak and wings.

Anna felt dizzy. There was an overpowering fragrance of lotus and hibiscus, sandalwood and joss sticks; gardens lush with lotus pools, bulbous-eyed koi peering from beneath water hyacinth and gibbons shrieking insults from their perches on ancient topiary. Orchids shaped like butterflies and human faces, and birds—turquoise kingfishers, Java sparrows, red-billed parakeets, and strutting peacocks. The cries of birds, and the sound of gongs and chanting and tinkling bells, flags streaming in the wind, and saffron-robed monks sprinkling the street with jasmine water—

And everywhere they looked, people were glaring back at them. It was too much. Anna closed her eyes, hands pressed against her cheeks. Beneath her the coach bounced and shook. And, at last, stopped.

From the driver's perch a voice echoed down faintly in Siamese. "The residence of the Kralahome."

"Yes—yes, *khawp khun*, thank you—," Anna stammered. She took Louis's hand and, summoning every ounce of strength that remained to her, smiled. "Come now, Louis, straighten your shirt. That's better. Moonshee, could you see that our things are sent ahead to our new house? And, Beebe, would you mind helping Louis down?"

They disembarked. In front of the Kralahome's residence a group of monks stopped their work and stared, some curiously, others with suspicion or disdain. Anna straightened, pushing a damp strand of hair from her hot cheeks. Without a word she swept inside.

A guard was expecting them, and ushered them upstairs to an open-air studio where rows of clerks sat at wide wooden tables, quill pens scratching furiously as they copied out letters and memos, all the minutiae of official correspondence. At the far end of the room a man stood on tiptoe, hanging an elaborately embroidered silk talisman from an archway.

At the sound of Anna's footsteps echoing through the room he turned, scrutinizing the newcomers. After a moment he tipped his head back.

"I am desiring to cleanse surroundings of evil spirits," he explained in English.

Anna darted a quick surprised glance at her son, then looked back at the man. In the room around them the sound of pen nib on paper had grown abruptly silent.

"I am interpreter," the man went on coldly. "Come. Your servants may wait here for you."

With a reassuring glance at her family, Anna followed him. The archway led into a huge chamber, its walls covered with silken hangings and the floor thick with Persian rugs. There were brass censors giving forth the sweet smell of incense, and man-size statues of Buddhas and other religious icons. In the corners stood several guards in the royal livery.

But the room was dominated by a low, round table fully twelve feet across, covered with papers. Behind this sat an imposing man, sharp-eyed and with a proud, hawkish face, smoking a long-stemmed pipe and perusing a stack of official documents. He stared at Anna with unabashed hauteur, smoke circling his head.

"Your Excellency." The interpreter stepped forward, then prostrated himself before the Kralahome. "May I present to you Mrs. Anna Leonowens. Mrs. Leonowens—His Excellency, Chao Phya Kralahome, Prime Minister of Siam."

A beat. The Kralahome continued to stare at Anna with penetrating eyes. She swallowed, waiting for him to speak, then curtsied. There was a quick exchange in Siamese between the Kralahome and his interpreter. Then the interpreter turned to her, still kneeling.

"Have you friends in Bangkok, sir?" he asked.

Anna shook her head, hands clasped in front of her. "No, I know no one here."

The interpreter relayed this information to the Kralahome, who studied her thoughtfully before asking another question.

"Sir is married?" the interpreter translated.

Anna unconsciously twisted her wedding ring. "I'm . . . a widow. And please, can you explain why you call me sir?"

The interpreter looked at her disdainfully. "Women do not stand in presence of His Excellency." He turned back to the Kralahome, who spoke again in Siamese, and once more translated for Anna. "How long are you in possession of dead husband?"

She hesitated. "Twenty-three months," she replied at last. The men said nothing but stared at her expectantly. "He—he was a captain in the British army."

The interpreter's disdain grew clearer. "And how did he die?"

Anna felt herself flush. She took a deep breath, forcing her voice to remain level, and said, "Could you please convey to His Excellency that my business here is as tutor to the King's eldest son, and it is not necessary for him to ask me any more personal questions?"

The interpreter regarded her hesitantly.

"Please?" Anna added in a softer voice.

Tentatively he turned back to the Prime Minister, who made a quick, sharp gesture of dismissal.

"In Siam, sir," the Kralahome announced with contempt, "it is custom to first ask questions of personal nature—to be polite."

Ignoring her embarrassment and shock at the realization that he knew English, the Kralahome turned his full attention back to the documents in front of him. The interpreter raised his hands in a *wai* of farewell, got to his feet, and began to usher Anna to the door. Abruptly she pulled away from him.

"Mr. Prime Minister! I assure you I meant no disrespect. However, getting here was something of a challenge."

The Kralahome did not glance up. "Sir will be shown to palace quarters."

"I'm sorry, but the King promised us a home of our own *outside* the palace," said Anna. "It is what was agreed upon."

"In Siam you will learn everything has its own time," the Kralahome replied tersely, still ignoring her.

Anna drew herself up. Then, pushing past the distressed interpreter, she marched to where the Kralahome sat, drew her letter from her bag, and shoved it under the Prime Minister's nose.

"I'm afraid that is quite unacceptable." She stabbed at the envelope with her finger. "Is this not the royal seal?"

Behind her the interpreter bobbed anxiously. Without so much as a glance at the letter, the Kralahome waved the man away, then shifted his steely gaze to Anna. She looked back at him uneasily.

"Sit," he commanded. When she hesitated he shouted, "Sit!"

She sat. Uncomfortably, on a narrow wooden bench a few feet from the Prime Minister, her skirts crinkling loudly as she settled herself, still trying to keep her gaze upon her imperious host.

"It is King's pleasure that you now reside in a royal household," the Kralahome snapped. "Why does sir object to live in palace?"

"I have many reasons, Your Excellency. However, equally important, an agreement was made, and agreements are meant to be kept. I have a letter from the King himself—"

She pulled out another envelope, much worn, its contents creased and furred from having been handled again and again, and gave it to the Kralahome. He eyed it warily, taking in the royal seal and familiar handwriting, then read it.

When he finished, the Kralahome handed the King's letter back to Anna. He drew deeply on his pipe. "Is sir aware there has been cholera in city?"

"I am no stranger to this part of the world, Your Excellency. There has been cholera everywhere we have lived, and we have learned to take precautions. But if the threat was as serious as you say, I am sure you would have sent someone to meet us at the ship."

The Kralahome's eyes narrowed, and in them Anna detected the faintest spark of respect.

"But," he said, "British or otherwise, you are merely woman."

With all due respect," she replied firmly, "in my country, the king *is* a woman. And *she* never breaks her promise."

Incensed, the Kralahome stood, glaring down at her with contempt.

"Refuting His Majesty is not done!" he cried.

Anna's heart pounded, but her voice was calm as she inclined her head. "Then perhaps I, who am not bound by your traditions, should see His Majesty now and remind him of our agreement."

The Kralahome stared at her incredulously. With a cry he turned and called out to the waiting guards, who stepped forward to escort Anna from the room.

"You will wait, schoolteacher, until King wish to see you, or you may go wherever sir pleases!"

And silently she was ushered from the room, to rejoin her family in their quarters in the palace.

24

two

I do not know what Mrs. Leonowens expected to find when she entered Bangkok, Krung Thep, our City of Great Angels. Certainly no Oriental fairytale land such as her countrymen read of in their storybooks and adventuring novels. My teacher had lived in both Bombay and Singapore, though I do not believe her tenure in either of those places could have most readily prepared her for her time with us.

Bangkok is a young capital, its official stature fewer than a hundred years old when Anna Leonowens arrived. As a child I remember the feverish intensity with which new buildings were being raised, and the excitement engendered by my father's pet projects. Turning an ancient elephant trail leading from the city into the New Road, so that my father's new

25

wheeled royal carriages could go back and forth, but also so that merchants could bring in teak from the forests; digging new canals; modernizing the military and police. With the aid of a friend who was an American missionary he created our first printing press. He did away with forced labor crews for public works, and created a royal mint so that we had coins with which to do business rather than strings of cowrie shells.

All of this, of course, was after he had spent much of his life in the monastery, living and praying as his brother monks did. He was fourteen when he took his vows—scarcely older than I was when I met Mrs. Leonowens—and he spent nearly thirty years wearing the saffron robe of a Buddhist monk, walking across our country with his brethren, owning only his wooden sandals and his robe and the wooden bowl from which he ate.

It was this life, more than any formal schooling, that prepared him for what was to come. Because as a monk he saw our people, in villages and rice fields, cities and temples. He saw them, but more than that, he knew them. They fed him; they spoke with him; they prayed with him, and for him, and alongside him. He met as well many other people: Christian *missionaries and Jesuits, the bishop who befriended him and taught him Latin, the European ambassadors who shared with him news of the world beyond Siam's borders.*

And so it was that when my father finally did take the throne, he was not a child-king, but a highly educated and introspective man of years. A man who had lived a life of poverty and contemplation, a man who had bent his passions toward learning and the sciences. And after his coronation, what set my father apart from his forefathers in the Chakri dynasty was the welcome that he extended to foreign interests from across the globe. This, of course, was to forestall the colonization which he had seen overtake our neighbors, but it was a noble and risky gesture all the same. It is a tribute to my father's bravery and extraordinary political acumen that his policies were a success, and made my own term as his successor as remarkable as it has been.

Still, I must admit that what I remember most about my father are his clocks. He had a passion for clocks, and every sort of Western timepiece—sundials, water clocks, tiny pocket watches, elaborate carven houses whose calm faces hid magically moving figures and shining gears. Anything mechanical, any-

27

thing that moved or helped to calculate the time, the seasons, the heavens—these were the things he loved. He had many concubines, and throngs of children, and the latter I can attest he loved with a full and generous heart.

But the one thing he loved as much as he did his children, was Knowledge. Science, Mathematics, Astronomy, Reason—these were his wives, his mistresses, his lovers. He took them to bed, he played with them, analyzed them, sometimes vented his fury upon them when he could make no sense of their arcane and often secret ways, but always he loved them, and surrounded himself with their issue—telescopes, microscopes, astrolabes, spectacles, gazing balls, barometers, thermometers, dioramas, vivariums, globes. He loved them to distraction, and like any good lover, above all he sought to understand that which he adored.

And, ultimately, it was one such lover that killed him. Although in truth, I do not believe he would have chosen another death.

three

Hours later, Anna was even more frustrated and exhausted.

"Don't bother unpacking, Beebe," she said, gesturing at the older woman as she struggled with yet another piece of their dented luggage. "It's only for the night."

Around them were all the remnants of their former life—broken valises and emptied cartons, her husband's uniform jacket draped over a chair, Louis's clothes and books neatly folded alongside a carven Buddha. They were in their quarters in the *Khang Nai*, or Forbidden Place, the hidden city within a city where the King's royal consorts and concubines lived with the children and servants. Several thousand people all told, and at this

29

moment Anna would gladly have challenged any one of them for a cool bath and a night's sleep. She sighed, handing a small parcel to Beebe, and declared, "This will be settled to our satisfaction or we will leave as soon as possible."

Behind her Louis sat within an arched window, staring out over a high tessellated wall overgrown with strangling vines. Beyond, in an unseen courtyard, scores of monks chanted, their voices rising and falling like the sound of distant waves. He glanced over his shoulder at his mother and said, "I thought we didn't have any money."

"Correct. But at this moment I do not need to be reminded of that."

Louis smiled meekly and gazed back out the window. "Sounds like we're living in a beehive."

Anna stepped over a pile of clothes. "First thing tomorrow I shall go directly to the King." She bent and angrily flipped open a trunk. "A monarch who refuses to keep his word is uncivilized, unenlightened, and, frankly, ungrateful. There are principles at stake," she went on, almost to herself. "And having a proper British household with some privacy is one of them."

Beebe nodded sympathetically. "I do not think Siam agrees with you, memsahib," she murmured.

Louis shook his head, puzzled. "But, Mother, how can it be a proper household when I've never even been to England? And you haven't lived there since you were a girl."

"India is British, Louis," said Anna in exasperation. "It has been for years. That's what being colonized is all about."

Moonshee and Beebe traded looks. "And that is what the King of Siam is all about," Moonshee whispered to his wife.

Outside, the chanting abruptly stopped. With one last peep over the wall, Louis clambered down from the window and back inside. "Well, all I can say is, Father would have put him right in his place."

Anna gave her son a sharp look. "Well, I'm very sorry I'm not the man your father was."

Louis stopped and stared up at her, hurt. Anna sighed. "I'm sorry, Louis. This—this is a good opportunity for us, and I . . . I suppose I should look at the positive side. Assuming there is one." She brushed the hair from his forehead and smiled. "Your father would have."

"He was a brave man, wasn't he?"

"Very. And most considerate, which is more than I can say for this—king."

She leaned forward to kiss him, then handed him a well-worn copy of the Bible. "Here. I did manage to find this. Now let's see if we can find your bed."

Gently she accompanied her son to the other room, to seek what comfort they could in the old, old tale of people lost in the wilderness, and to fall, at last, into anxious sleep.

Prince Chowfa did not sleep well that night, either. Evil dreams pursued him, of a river running red and grasping hands snaking down from the overhanging trees, hands that sought to strangle him where he sat upon the *howdah*, surveying the forest around him. When he woke within the small, steep-roofed house where they had decamped, it was with a profound sense of unease. Outside, sunlight was already beginning to stream through the gnarled masses of rhododendron and pines. Smoke rose from a cook fire, and in the distance a peacock pheasant croaked. Chowfa dressed hurriedly, barking commands to his assistants as he strode down the narrow steps to wait impatiently as the elephants were prepared for the day's journey.

They were near the village of Bang Pli. Chowfa, brother of the Siamese king, was leading his royal envoy on their inspection of the northern Siamese province of Chiang Mai. Burma was not more than a day's march away, and there had been rumors of incursions by Burmese troops. As of yet Prince Chowfa had found no evidence to support these claims—there were always rumors, and always those who found their promulgation to be of political or personal benefit. Still, the latest news from the region had been disturbing enough that Prince Chowfa thought a visit to the governor was in order. Last night's dreams only increased his sense of urgency. By the time their procession began heading northward once again, it was still early enough that they could reach the governor's mansion, complete their business, and, assuming the rumors were no more than that, enjoy a sumptuous evening meal—the governor prided himself on keeping a fine kitchen even in so remote a spot.

"Sir! Sir!"

Prince Chowfa looked around, steadying himself with one hand upon the *howdah*, then glanced down at the forest floor.

"Yes?" he called out. "What is it?"

"Sir—!"

A man came running from the trees onto the wide

trail where the royal procession of elephants and foot soldiers formed a line nearly a quarter-mile long. "Halt!" Prince Chowfa called to his elephant handler, then bade the running man come closer. "What is it?"

"The governor's mansion—sir—I am employed there. Yesterday eve I was sent to meet a trade convoy on the river, as is customary. But at dawn I returned and—and—"

His voice broke, and Prince Chowfa stared down in concern. The man's clothes were torn, his body streaked with blood and soot. Quickly Prince Chowfa turned and gestured for assistance. "Has something happened to the governor?" he cried.

"Sir, we are overtaken . . ." the man replied, and collapsed.

"You down there! Assist him!" shouted Prince Chowfa. "Bring him to me when we have reached the governor's residence! Now! Hurry!"

It was another hour before they arrived. Even then Prince Chowfa smelled the clearing before it came into view. He withdrew a silken handkerchief and covered his nose and face, steeling himself for what he feared awaited him.

It was worse than he could have imagined. A lifetime of overseeing the military needs of his country had inured him to much, but even so he gasped. The mansion was in ruins, burned to the ground with nothing remaining but heaps of smoldering timbers, with here and there a blackened form twisted into a tortured semblance of life: a clawed hand reaching for a shattered chandelier, a silver betel-nut box balanced upon a child's skull. Prince Chowfa shouted at his steed to head toward what had been the mansion's rear veranda. The elephant obeyed, huge feet heedlessly crushing ash and dead embers, matted piles of wet clothing and broken glass.

"My lord—Prince Chowfa—"

The Prince turned his head, only his dark eyes visible above the handkerchief. On the ground, one of his men stood and pointed at a large banyan tree, several yards from what had been a garden. From one of the banyan's great branches hung a dozen forms. Their clothes were incongruously festive, crimson and gold and green. It was the governor's family, clad in their finest robes: news of the coming royal procession must have reached them. But their faces were nearly unrecognizable beneath the grim traces of decay that had already begun to claim them in the tropical heat. On the ground beneath the contents of the mansion were scattered trunks and treasure boxes and serving platters, broken so that their contents spilled across the earth in a litter of smashed melons and brass trays, scrolls and lacquered baskets. Strewn amidst these were the governor's servants, their throats slashed and limbs severed, blood staining the fine silks and furnishings they had been carrying.

"Governor Bunnang and his family," Prince Chowfa's sergeant cried. "Even the children, Lord—they even took the—"

"I can see what they did." Rage burned through compassion as the Prince took in the three smallest figures on the tree. "Cut them down! Prepare them for burning immediately, so that their souls may be released!"

"Lord . . ."

A faint voice trembled from an overgrown copse of trees. Prince Chowfa's hand leapt to his sword, but even as a group of soldiers rushed forward, a wizened man crept from beneath the greenery, followed by an ancient white-haired woman and perhaps a score of terrified children. The Prince looked down at them, his heart aching. He withdrew the handkerchief from his face and slowly began to speak.

"People of Bang Pli—Governor Bunnang was a loyal friend to my brother, his majesty King Mongkut, and I promise we will find these cowards who dare spill Siam's blood."

He searched the faces in the crowd, finally settled on the first woman who had appeared. "You. What happened here?"

The woman raised her shaking hands, held palm to palm, and bowed. "Burmese soldiers, Your Highness. They said if we cut them down, they would return . . ."

Prince Chowfa's mouth tightened. "It is as I thought," he said in a low voice. He looked over his shoulder at the elephant behind him, where his second-in-command sat bolt upright, staring in disgust and fury at the ruins. "Send word to my brother. We need reinforcements—now."

With a cry Prince Chowfa urged his mount onward, the villagers trailing after his retinue like fallen leaves borne off by a flood-swollen stream.

Weeks passed. In the spacious palace suite occupied by Anna and her family, the valises had long since been unpacked, their hoard of woefully inappropriate clothes—layers of linen undergarments, Louis's

37

woolen suits, Anna's silks and cambric dresses—now hanging limp and reproachful in a sandalwood armoire. Beebe and Moonshee, accustomed to both change and the glacial pace at which it could take place, made the easiest transition. King or no king, they had their own offices to perform. Their days were filled with all the work of keeping house for Mrs. Leonowens, and learning to make do with what Siam gave them: orchids for the dining table, anchovies instead of kippers for breakfast, Louis's cricket bat instead of a bamboo rug beater.

Louis himself found much to occupy his days. He still had his studies—one of the great disadvantages of having a parent for a teacher was that he never, ever really went on vacation—but he also had all of the magical city within a city to explore. And so he did, endlessly, relentlessly, so that it seemed sometimes that he could not recall whether he had actually seen a thing—a five-headed dragon gondola cresting across a lotus-studded *klong*, a snake with eyes like rubies crowning a naked child with blood-stained lips—or dreamed it.

Anna, on the other hand, knew it was not a dream. As the weeks droned on, she grew more and more impatient, but tried for Louis's sake to retain the outward calm and poise he had grown up with. She sat now within the scant shade of a small pagoda-shaped pavilion, reading for the hundredth time the well-worn pages of her Siamese primer.

"Sir?"

Anna closed her book and looked up. Just outside the pavilion stood the interpreter. His uncomfortable expression was also now familiar to her; she nodded, waiting for this aftenoon's excuse.

"Sir, His Excellency regrets that His Majesty, King Mongkut, is unable to met with you today. But soon. Very soon."

Anna's lips tightened in a thin smile. She turned to look across the wide boulevard, to where the Kralahome stood upon his terrace, puffing his pipe and staring down at them. She stared back, feeling blood rise angrily to her cheeks, then looked at the interpreter.

"Please inform His Excellency that his use of the word *soon* is inaccurate," she said coldly. "It means 'in a timely manner,' which, in my case, obviously no longer applies."

But the next morning, surprising news reached Anna.

"Sir. You are to accompany me now—"

"Now?" She stared across the breakfast table to where the interpreter stood in the doorway, flanked by an irate-looking Moonshee. "But we've just—"

"If you please, sir—it is now, or—"

"Yes! Yes, of course!" In a flurry of silk and lace, Anna jumped up, nearly upsetting the table. "Louis! Moonshee, I'll need my bag! Louis, there you are—come, brush your hair—oh, never mind, there's no time! We're going."

"Now?" Louis stared at her, dumbfounded.

"Yes! Yes—!" Anna grabbed his hand and hurried out into the morning sun. In front of them, the interpreter's slender form was already heading at a near run toward the Audience Hall. "We're going to meet the King."

The Kralahome and his entourage met them at the entrance to the Grand Hall. "Unfortunate your meeting so delayed, sir," the Kralahome said brusquely, tilting his head toward the archway. "King's obligations reach into every corner of Siam."

Anna nodded. "It gave me time to think about many things, Your Excellency, including why you pretended not to speak English."

The Kralahome gave her a shrewd look. "I have learned it wise to be cautious."

Anna smiled. "Then we will assume our speaking now is a step forward."

"Best not to assume too much." He stepped through the arch. "When presented to His Majesty, you and son will remember to touch forehead to floor."

"Your Excellency." Anna drew herself up, giving Louis a quick sideways look. "Although we have become better acquainted with your customs, we have not forgotten our own."

"Then, how shall you greet him?" the Kralahome asked warily.

"With the utmost respect."

They proceeded down the broad marble steps, onto a balcony looking into a sumptuous room whose walls were covered with silk tapestries and carvings depicting every imaginable sort of elegance: flowers, hunting scenes, demons and deities, and men in Victorian garb. Through a long window could be glimpsed the still blue depths of the beautiful ornamental lake that stretched outside, dragon-shaped canoes plying its surface. A blood-colored carpet flowed across the expanse of floor, and thronged upon it were prostrate noblemen and courtiers, all facing a raised dais where sat the most imposing figure Anna had ever seen—

Phra Chom Klao, the ruler known to the Western world as King Mongkut of Siam.

She took a breath, heart pounding, and stepped to the edge of the balcony. Below her the King stared imperiously from his throne—a tall man, powerfully built, his black hair close-cropped, his features angular but not harsh. It was a face that radiated an intense but reserved intelligence: she thought of a certain chess master at his game, observing his opponent's move as he prepared his own. Even from this distance she could see his eyes darting restlessly between the men who stood before him. And for the moment, Anna was very happy not to be subjected to that lightning gaze.

Anna started as the Kralahome's voice sounded softly in her ear. "The man to right of His Majesty is Consul-General Alak."

The Kralahome pointed at a highly decorated, muscular officer scowling at a European man who stood nervously on the carpet. "The *farang* is the French emissary. And the others behind His Majesty are his bodyguards, Nikorn, Noi, and Pitak," the Kralahome finished, indicating three colossal figures with shaven heads and imperturbable expressions.

Anna watched, fascinated. The French emissary

stepped forward, bowing as he presented the King with a gorgeous jewel-encrusted sword, its hilt declared with sapphire and gold fleur-de-lis.

"Look at that sword!" whispered Louis.

Anna nodded, listening as the unctuous French diplomat gave a long, rambling speech in his own tongue.

"It's a gift," she whispered back. "Apparently a French warship ran aground where it shouldn't have been."

On his throne, King Mongkut sat, staring at the diplomat with cool appraisal. After a minute he delivered a clipped command to his interpreter, who stepped forward and accepted the sword, replying to the diplomat in French. The King's assistant, a tall man in official regalia, clapped his hands. A gong tolled loudly, and in the very back of the Audience Hall noblemen made their farewell *wais* and began to depart. The Kralahome turned to Anna.

"It appears sir must wait to meet His Majesty another day."

Taken aback, Anna stared at the Prime Minister, then glanced back down to where King Mongkut stood, preparing to leave. Her voice shook slightly as she said, "No, I do not think so."

She grabbed Louis's hand, hurrying down the steps toward the throne. The Kralahome stared after her, astonished, then hastily followed. Her footsteps gave back a muffled echo as she marched to the dais the King had just left. In her wake, those still lying prostrate on the floor peeked after the mad *farang* in amazement.

"Your Majesty." Anna sank into a deep curtsy. Beside her, Louis bowed. "My name is Anna Leonowens."

King Mongkut had almost reached his chamber doors when the voice stopped him. He turned, shocked by the interruption. Anna had risen from her curtsy and was walking toward him. With a soft cry, the three bodyguards leapt in front of their master, swords drawn to block her approach.

Anna smiled disarmingly. "I am the school—"

"*Stop!!!*"

Startled, Anna did just that. Louis dropped to the floor and covered his head.

"Who?" the King cried. "*Who?*"

Through the audience, heads slowly lifted as everyone strove to see the woman who dared stand before the King. The incensed Kralahome drew up alongside Anna and immediately prostrated himself. Still staring at her in disbelief, the King stepped forward.

"Who?!" he repeated.

"Your Majesty," said the Kralahome. "May I present Mem Anna Leonowens and son, Louis."

Anna turned, looking for Louis, and pulled him to his feet. "You Majesty," she said, "I have been kept waiting for three weeks. And while I respect that you have issues of great importance—"

"*Silence!*" The King stared furiously at the Kralahome. "Has she no understanding of protocol?"

"She had been advised."

The bodyguards parted as the King drew himself up directly alongside Anna. She stared back at him, flushed; but as he held her gaze, she saw his own alter somewhat—from rage to something less threatening.

The King was intrigued.

"You are teacher?" he said at last.

"I am, yes," said Anna, flustered.

"You do not look sufficient of age for scientific teaching. How many years have you?"

Anna fought to maintain her composure. "Enough to know that age and wisdom do not necessarily go hand in hand, Your Majesty."

The King's eyes narrowed. He considered whether or not to return this volley, then:

"I doubt you would say same for being bold and English."

Anna smiled ruefully. "They are rather inseparable, I'm afraid."

The King nodded at this small sign of humility. Then he abruptly spun on his heel and walked through the outer door, his retinue scurrying after him. In the Audience Hall a huge rippling sigh echoed, as a hundred courtiers exhaled and got to their feet. The Kralahome stood along with the rest and glared at the confused schoolteacher.

"His Majesty has not dismissed you!" he cried, pointing after the King. "Follow him!"

Anna and Louis fairly ran. Down a long, narrow passage lined with ancient murals, where an endless line of shriveled duennas and *wai*ing servants bowed as their king passed.

"You articulate logical answer under pressure, Mem Leonowens," Monkut pronounced without looking at her.

"That is very kind of—," panted Anna.

"—but irritating superior attitude King find most unbeautiful. However, it will serve you well given decision I now make."

"Your Majesty," Anna stammered, "please, first

impressions can often be very misleading . . ."

They reached a pair of massive double doors, of red-stained wood heavily carved with sinuous vines and lotus blossoms. To each side of the doors stood a towering statue of a demon guardian, and beside each of these stood an Amazon guard. The guards did not blink as the King strode up to them, gesturing as he announced, "Along with Prince Chulalongkorn, you shall now teach all my children."

He turned to Anna. "Come!"

Without a sound the guards pushed open the great doors. Anna tried not to gasp, but Louis was less practiced at hiding his amazement: he cried out softly as the King bade them enter the Children's Garden.

"Oh, my goodness," murmured Anna.

It was as though one of the gorgeous jeweled carvings of the Ramakien had come to life. Everywhere were exquisitely manicured trees, topiary statues of birds and fantastic animals, huge porcelain vases overflowing with hibiscus and purple orchids, palm leaves and scarlet amaryllis. Fountains purled and wept; goggle-eyed ornamental koi swam in pools strewn with lily pads and water hyacinth that smelled of oranges.

47

But most marvelous of all was that the landscape was alive—with children. Running, laughing, playing children, none older than eleven, darting in and out of red-lacquered pavilions, clambering up the elaborately tended trees as their nurses chased them, playing tag and hide-and-seek and croquet, stroking a litter of dark-eyed Siamese kittens. Twins capered around a pool, riding make-believe horses of woven banana leaves, while a solitary girl dropped rose petals on the water's calm surface.

And watching over them all were their mothers—the *Chao Chom Manda*, Mothers of Royal Children; and concubines, even more brilliantly clad than their sons and daughters in cloth-of-gold and Chinese silks, brocaded robes, and elegantly simple *jongkrabanes*. Most of the women wore their hair cropped short, save for a small topknot; a few still had long black plaits. Several held infants and nursed them unselfconsciously. Others, not much more than children themselves, laughed and joined in the games.

"Twenty-three wives, forty-two concubines, fifty-eight offspring, and ten more on the way. Each unique," said King Mongkut proudly. "Each one my hope for the future."

swallowed, averting her eyes as a woman

laughed and parted her silken blouse, exposing a breast for her infant to nurse from. The Englishwoman's expression was not lost on the King.

"I understand your surprise," he said with a meaningful glance. "Not as many as emperor of China, but he did not spend half of life in monastery."

He turned and gazed fondly at the woman nursing his infant son, and said, "King making up for lost time."

Louis stared openmouthed, then tugged at his mother's sleeve. "Mother, what's a concubine?"

Before she could answer a gong sounded, deafeningly. Like startled antelope, everyone in the garden froze and turned, seeing the King. With near-military precision they dropped to the ground, foreheads pressed to the grass. The King regarded them measuringly and clapped his hands.

"Attention, my most blessed and royal family! We have company. Two who have sailed from far, far away."

Once more the assemblage touched their heads to the ground. King Mongkut smiled benignly. Then, motioning Anna and Louis to follow, he began walking through the prostrate crowd. As he passed, children raised their heads furtively, staring at the strangers, while Anna and her son gazed enchanted at the beautifully dressed, and even more beautifully behaved, royal children.

At the end of a winding path the King stopped, gazing approvingly at a boy lying prostrate before him. As though some unspoken signal had passed between them, the boy got to his feet. In his face was none of the servility or urgency that colored most others who stood before the King. Indeed, he gave his father only a curt nod before turning to stare with open contempt at Louis. The two boys were roughly the same age and the same height. But the Siamese boy was clad in an ivory-colored white blouson and gold-braided belt, the richness of his clothes offset by his disdainful expression. The King extended his hand, tilting his head toward Anna.

"Presenting Original Pupil and Heir Apparent, Prince Chulalongkorn. And this, my son, is your new teacher."

Anna bowed graciously to the boy. "Your Highness, I am deeply honored."

The crown prince gaped at her, then turned to his father, astonished.

"Have I done something to offend you?" he pleaded in Siamese.

The King frowned. "Of course not."

"Then why do you punish me with imperialist schoolteacher?"

Louis took in the other boy's sullen face. He didn't need to understand Siamese to read his expression, or the disdain in the Prince's words. He tugged at his mother's hand again and whispered, "He doesn't look too happy about it."

King Mongkut looked down at his son. After a moment he nodded and turned back to the rest of his family, still lying upon the garden floor.

"Dearest family! I desire you all, when of appropriate age, to be educated in English language, science, and literature."

He paused, for Chulalongkorn's benefit, then went on, "This is a necessary and practical gift I give to you, and you must never forget to respect your renowned teacher"—he gestured dramatically— "Mem Anna Leonowens."

Anna bit her lip, staring at the scores of people whose numbers indicated just how impressively— and unexpectedly—her teaching duties had grown. She took a breath, then spoke in halting Siamese.

"Hello. I am very pleased to meet you. This is my son, Louis."

From the garden came a susurrus of whispers and soft laughter. Several of the concubines reached for each other, pointing surreptitiously at the Englishwoman and giggling. The King chuckled.

"You are first *farang* they have seen. They are wondering if you might have more children hiding under your skirt. In time, you shall teach them as well."

He turned and pointed at a gold-encrusted pavilion surrounded by magnolia trees hung with birdcages. "Oh! Must not forget head wife: the Lady Thiang. It is my pleasure that you help make her fine scholar, too."

From the pavilion stepped a woman in her late thirties, still formidably beautiful, her kind eyes shot through with an acute intelligence. She joined her husband, *wai*ing deeply to Anna as she greeted her.

"Welcome, Mem teacher."

Anna curtsied back. "Thank you, Lady Thiang."

With an appreciative nod the King began quickly to recite a litany of names. "Prince Thingkon Yai, Prince Suk Sawat, Princess Kannika Kaeo . . .

As he spoke, each child rose and made a respectful *wai* to Anna. She nodded, smiling, tried to recall their names but after a minute or two gave up. There were so many of them!

"Prince Cho-thai—"

Suddenly a small unripe mangosteen bounced off the King's head. Anna started; the King looked up, scowling with mock ferocity. Hanging from the magnolia behind them was a tiny girl in white, giggling uncontrollably.

"And the Princess Fa-Ying," the King finished, his scowl turning to a rapturous smile. He opened his arms, and with another giggle Fa-Ying dropped fearlessly into them.

"I am not princess. I am monkey!" she cried—in English.

The King bowed. "My deepest apologies, *looja*." Gently he put her down, the little girl hugging his legs. "Her true name Chanthara Monthon, but everyone call her Fa-Ying, 'Celestial Princess.'" He made a face, and Fa-Ying giggled. "I study her in English myself," he explained to Anna.

"Your Majesty . . ." Anna turned, taking in the watchful children, their curious mothers and nursemaids, Prince Chulalongkorn frowning with none of his father's beneficence. "I am most flattered by your welcome, and I find the opportunity to begin a school an exciting one." She hesitated before adding, "Such devotion to progress is to be commended."

She glanced behind her at the Kralahome, recalling that there were still those in Siam who believed "progress" to be a crime against the state. The Kralahome gazed back at her coolly, his expression unreadable, but King Mongkut was already nodding in agreement.

"Reform is vital to my country's survival," he said. "This have I seen, in my studies in the monastery, in my visits with *farangs* and my present duties with ambassadors. But reform must be slow, not to disrupt existing order."

He looked down at Princess Fa-Ying, standing barefoot at his side and beaming up at him, smiled, and went on. "As tiny feet change, so too will Siam."

Anna smiled too, then lifted her head to gaze fearlessly into the King's eyes. "But, Your Majesty—being in a country with so many unique customs, I must feel free to follow our own traditions if I am to raise my son to be like his father, which I very much hope he will be."

The King met her gaze. "As father, I understand."

"Then Your Majesty realizes why having a home outside the palace is of such importance to me," she went on quickly. "A home which has been promised but has, so far, not been provided."

The King tilted his head. "It is my pleasure that you live in the palace," he said firmly.

Anna's resolve echoed his own. "But it is not mine, Your Majesty."

The King's eyes flashed. He stepped toward her, his voice booming across the tranquil garden. "You *do not* set conditions of your employment and *you shall obey*!"

Trembling, Louis slipped behind his mother, while all across the garden the royal children hid their eyes at the sight of their father's rage. Only Anna stood, shaken but refusing to give in as she stared back at the King. "May I respectfully remind His Majesty that I am not his servant, but his 'guest.'"

For a long, tense moment their eyes were locked. Then:

"A guest who is paid," the King said tersely. "Education begins tomorrow."

He turned and headed back to the gate.

"And what of our house?" Anna cried after him.

Without looking back, he replied, "Everything has its own time."

Silently the garden's vast gates swung open once more, just as silently closed after him. The King was gone. Anna stared, angry yet resolute, at the doors, completely unaware of the hundreds of eyes gazing at her in unrestrained awe and amazement.

A woman—a woman!—had talked back to their King!

In their little Siamese house that evening, Anna stood before the vanity, sighing with pleasure as she dabbed cool water on her cheeks. At her elbow, the worn tintype image of her husband in his dress uniform leaned against the wall. Anna finished her ablutions, dried her face on a square of thick cotton, and gave the tintype a wry salute.

"You would not have believed your eyes!" Louis's voice echoed to her from the adjoining bedroom. Smiling, Anna peered out to see her son jumping onto his bed and neatly avoiding Moonshee as the old man unfurled mosquito netting in his familiar nightly ritual. "She looked right at him, and then his voice boomed, *You shall obey!*'"

Louis's voice cracked as he imitated the King. Moonshee laughed, shaking his head and shooing the boy from the bed. "Get your nightclothes, young sir—"

"Just like that!" Louis went on excitedly. "And Mother didn't even bat an eye!"

"I would have, had I not been so frightened," Anna called out, shuddering a little at the memory.

"No wonder people crawl around in front of him," said Moonshee.

Behind her, Beebe entered with clean linens. "He sounds dreadful," the old woman said.

Anna nodded. "He did unnerve me, I must say."

Louis had by now leapt from the bed and settled himself on a trunk, there to watch Moonshee finish with the mosquito netting. For several minutes he sat thoughtfully with his chin cupped in his hands, and finally asked, "Moonshee, why does the King have so many wives?"

His mother and Beebe exchanged looks. "Because heathens obviously lack restraint," whispered Anna.

"That is an excellent question," Moonshee replied loudly. "For your mother."

Louis hopped to his feet. "Mother?" Anna looked at Beebe, trying to frame an answer. "Mother . . . ?"

"I heard you, Louis." She cleared her throat, all too aware of the uniformed man staring out from his tintype, all the weight of the empire in his eternal

57

unblinking gaze. "Well . . . Siam is a monarchy, just like we have in England. So the power of the throne is passed on from parent to child, just as it is at home. But even royal children are threatened by disease—cholera and smallpox and the like—and there is always the danger of war. And so one way a royal family maintains its control of the throne, in the face of these dangers, is to have as many children as possible."

Louis's face brightened. "So he needs a lot of wives to take care of them?"

Relief flooded Anna. "A keen observation, dear. Now off to bed."

She kissed him good night. Louis started for his bed, stopped. "Does he . . . does he love all of them?"

Anna hesitated. "In a way."

"Like you loved Father?"

Anna smiled wistfully. "Things are very different here, Louis. Even love . . ."

She kissed him again, then spun him around and pushed him toward the bed. Beebe and Moonshee shot her amused looks, and Anna turned away, hiding a smile. After a moment Louis called out from the other room.

"Mother, why doesn't Queen Victoria have a lot of husbands?"

The three grown-ups froze. Then Anna raised her voice and answered in a tone that even Queen Victoria would have obeyed:

"Good *night*, Louis."

four

The next morning dawned clear and surprisingly cool, the sky a deep lacquered blue beyond the spires and glittering towers of the palace. Anna stirred early, still buoyed by her encounter with the King. The air smelled sweetly fragrant from Moonshee's jasmine incense, mingled with the familiar, bracingly pungent scent of the carbolic soap she'd brought with them from India and the odor of frangipani. It all conspired to send Anna into that serene twilight state between sleeping and wakefulness. For some minutes she lay in bed, the mosquito netting moving slowly back and forth above her, as though she were still aboard the *Newcastle*.

But the sound of chanting from the monastery

and the sharp mewling cries of peafowl quickly put the lie to *that* thought. With a groan Anna roused herself, calling to Louis to wake up, and began to dress.

"What will we do today, Mother?" Louis asked a short time later.

Anna looked up over her breakfast—fresh mangos and shaved coconut, a sort of rice porridge which was the closest Beebe could come to good plain English oatmeal. "Well," she said slowly, "I'd thought we could go back to the Kralahome and see if he'd any directives as to what, precisely, I should be doing with myself."

"Oh." Louis looked disappointed. "You mean, you won't be arguing with the King again?"

Anna suppressed a smile. "I should think not!"

"Not today, at least," countered Beebe. "Even the King needs a day off sometimes."

After breakfast, Anna and Louis gathered their things and prepared for an outing. "Take your books," Anna said, picking up her own battered primer and a copy of the *Webster's Speller* in its distinctive blue binding. "I think first we will go back to the Children's Garden—I would like to speak to Lady Thiang again. She, at least, might have some idea of what I must do with all those children."

And of what I'm up against with their father, Anna thought, with a farewell glance at her husband's tin-type portrait. She touched her hair, its braids neatly pinned above the nape of her neck, adjusted the wide sweep of her silken hoop skirt, and marched determinedly from their little palace apartment.

They followed a series of curving paths to the wide avenue outside the Grand Palace, passing slaves and servants, bands of monks in their bright yellow robes, men bearing twittering sparrows in bamboo cages and old women carrying baskets from which live eels dangled like so many coils of rope. It was enough to entertain any ordinary English child for a month of Sundays, and Louis's round, rosy face grew even pinker as he stopped to gape at a boy no older than himself, leading a young elephant by a golden cord.

"Mother! Look, Mother! Can I—"

"*No*," said Anna firmly, and took him by the hand. "You most certainly may *not*."

They hurried on, past high walls overgrown with pink-flowering vines, past perfumed fountains and ancient statues where geckos like beaded purses sat and regarded Louis with wide golden eyes. At the entrance to the broad avenue leading to the Grand Palace, Anna stopped.

"Now, what is *this*?" she wondered aloud.

In front of them the avenue was crowded with people. The usual mob of merchants, visiting diplomats, servants, and gardeners, but also a throng of onlookers as open in their amazement as Louis. Anna frowned, trying to see above the head and shoulders of a man carrying a huge wicker basket filled with bird's nests, collected for soup. The man cried out to a friend, moving aside, and Anna quickly took his place, dragging Louis after her.

"What is it? Mother?" Above the throng a sedan chair bobbed, carried by four bare-chested men who towered above the others. Yet the chair seemed more a miniature temple than a mode of conveyance: its high, scalloped roof so brilliantly gilded, it looked as though it were aflame, its walls encrusted with jewels and tiny carven dragons of onyx and alabaster and cinnabar. Heavy curtains of gold jacquard hid the chair's occupant, as though it were an enchanted theater whose actors had yet to awaken from some binding spell.

But as the sedan chair jostled past Anna, two slender arms heavily weighted with golden ornaments emerged, parting the drapes. An excited murmur ran through the people thronging the avenue. And, despite herself, Anna joined in.

"Ooh . . ."

From her moving perch above the crowd gazed a beautiful young noblewoman. Her slim body was clad in cloud-colored silk brocade, embroidered with pearls and gold filigree. Her mouth was carefully outlined in red, her eyebrows shaped with black charcoal, and on her head rested a crown of poppies made of hammered gold, each holding within its heart a single glowing ruby.

But the meticulously drawn curve of her lips could not disguise that the woman was not smiling, and her oblique black eyes beneath their arching brows were immeasurably sad. Anna clutched her books to her breast like a schoolgirl, staring raptly at the lovely, disconsolate figure in her curtained cage. So intent was she that Anna did not see the distraught young man darting in and out of the crowd, his eyes fixed upon the noblewoman's; nor did she hear his low urgent voice, calling out to the woman as she was borne toward the palace by the King's slaves.

"Who was that?" whispered Louis.

Anna said nothing, only continued to stare. And then slowly, oh so slowly, the young woman's head turned. The golden poppies nodded in the breeze as she stared back at Anna. For an instant their gazes held and locked, and Anna had the irrevocable sense that she was, somehow, still half-asleep beneath the gauzy curtain of mosquito netting: because surely no mortal woman could be so lovely and proud and sad, and surely no woman would ever gaze thus at Anna Leonowens, as though deep into the Englishwoman's hidden heart, and see there Anna's own sorrow, her loss and yearning for what was forever out of reach.

Then the moment was gone. The slaves hastened their pace; the sedan chair bounced over a mound in the road and abruptly disappeared behind a living wall of onlookers.

"Who was that?" Louis repeated, his eyes wide and rapt.

"I—I don't know," said Anna. She shook her head, as though awakening from a long, troubled sleep. Before them the crowd had moved on, following the procession. Where a band of silent monks had stood, she could now clearly see another pair of massive double doors, the mates of those inside the palace that led to the Children's Garden. Anna took a deep breath, quickly patted her hair, and gave Louis a cursory inspection, straightening his collar.

"Now, I'm not certain if they will be expecting us again so soon. And remember, darling, *we're* the foreigners."

She raised her hand, placed it upon one of the doors, and entered.

Inside, all was as it had been the day before, save *that* had been a garden in luminous motion, and *this* was a garden still and solemn as a plum-blossom painting. Beneath the cluster of pavilions the King's children stood in utter silence, each one holding a slate and a *Webster's Speller*. They were lined up according to age, with the tiny Fa-Ying beaming at one end of the garden and her brother, Prince Chu-lalongkorn, scowling at the other. Beside him, fixing Anna with her enigmatic gaze, was the Lady Thiang.

"Presenting royal school, sir," she said, bowing gracefully. "Building real name, Temple of the Mothers of the Free. But for you now—school."

Anna stared at the children, speechless. After all

these weeks—a school at last! It was almost too good to be true.

"Anything is wrong, sir?" Lady Thiang asked with an anxious look.

"No, Lady Thiang." Anna smiled. "Nothing at all."

She walked past them, like a general inspecting her ranks, and entered the largest pavilion. Here rows of desks had been arranged, with a single long teakwood table at the front of the room and another, higher table angled off it nearby. Alongside this five slaves stood at attention, woven fans held high. Anna gave them a curious look, then crossed to her desk, admiring the brand-new chalkboards hung behind it and the array of neatly stacked textbooks, writing folders, and bundles of pencils that awaited her students.

"My!" she exclaimed. "This is more like it."

In the door of the pavilion, Lady Thiang nodded. Excitedly the children hurried in, Prince Chula-longkorn at the head of the line. He made his way to the highest desk, ignoring the servants who began immediately to fan him. The other children grouped themselves at their own desks, whispering and exchanging looks as they stood. Louis came last of all, self-consciously waiting at the desk across from the dour young Prince and his retinue.

"Well," said Anna, squaring her shoulders and staring out at her charges. "I suppose class is now in session."

She gestured for them to sit, and they did—all except for the Crown Prince. He stepped forward, head erect, and pronounced in careful English, "Greetings, Mem Leonowens. My father wish to give sir this to put on path of good teaching."

He clapped his hands, and from the back of the pavilion a servant began to crawl, bearing a large scroll. Louis stared, dumbfounded, as the man crept all the way to where Anna stood, torn between embarrassment and self-control. The servant extended the scroll, still not raising his eyes from the floor. Anna took the parchment curiously and unrolled it.

It was a map of Siam, borders drawn in spidery green ink and with Siamese characters floating across mountains and seas like so many royal pennons. In the very center of the map was a likeness of King Mongkut. A fair likeness, Anna thought, except for its unsettling resemblance to certain of the demonic temple carvings that stood guard outside the Grand Palace.

"Thank you, Your Highness," she said, inclining her head to the Prince. "I shall do my best to keep that in mind, and may I compliment you on your English."

Prince Chulalongkorn lifted his chin proudly. "Siam, population six million, spreading across forty-nine bountiful provinces, from Burma in west to Cambodia in east. All presided over by King Maha Mongkut, Lord of Life, whose strength and power reach everywhere."

At this, all the royal children smiled and nodded knowingly. Louis looked at the map, then at his mother. Unable to resist a joke, he said, "Not in *my* house they don't."

Chulalongkorn turned to him haughtily. "Son of teacher is forgetting—*I* am son of king."

The younger boy shrank back, embarrassed. "Son of teacher could care less."

"You will sit somewhere else!" the Crown Prince thundered.

"I will not!"

"Louis," Anna said warningly. "Remember what I said . . ."

Louis turned to her, red-faced but calm. "Sorry, Mother, but he started it."

Anna glanced at Lady Thiang, whose own eyes were fixed on the Prince's. Chulalongkorn was glaring at Louis, who stared back unafraid.

"In my country," the Prince shouted, "man never tell woman he is sorry about anything, ever! If you had father, you would know that."

With a muffled cry Louis jumped to his feet. Before Anna could take a step, he raced at the future king of Siam and gave him a good solid push.

"*You* don't have a father! You have a *map!*"

"Louis!" cried Anna.

Prince Chulalongkorn quivered with rage. "*It is forbidden to touch Royalty!*"

"I didn't touch you—I shoved you! Why don't you get one of your slaves to shove me back?"

And fast as a striking cobra, he flung himself upon the older boy. The Crown Prince went down, punching and kicking as Louis pounded at his chest. With shrieks of excitement the royal children swarmed from their seats, crawling over each other in their haste to cheer their brother on.

"Louis! Your Highness! *No!*"

Anna pushed the other children aside and tried to separate the boys, but it was hopeless. They were locked together like two fighting stag beetles, rolling on the ground and knocking over chairs, sending books flying as they flailed at each other. Lady Thiang joined in, struggling to pull Prince Chulalongkorn free and getting her dress torn in the process.

"Louis, stop this *instant*—," Anna panted. Behind her, a single small figure jumped up from the melee and scampered from the pavilion, heading for the double gates that opened into the palace—

Princess Fa-Ying. She ran breathlessly down the corridor, ignoring the looks of the Amazon guards as she headed straight for the Audience Hall. Here too she passed unchecked—the King's own guards were accustomed to Fa-Ying's intrusions—and paused only when she stood safely within the Great Hall itself, trying to catch her breath.

"The nobleman, Thak Chaloemtiarana," an interpreter was intoning. On the dais at the front of the hall, her father sat, surrounded by his bodyguards. Before him a beautiful woman knelt upon the floor, head bowed beneath the weight of a crown of golden poppies. To either side of her, slaves in crimson robes held up the branches of ornately jeweled trees, their stems made of ivory, their leaves of gold and jade threaded with pearls. ". . . *Siam's*

most prosperous tea merchant, who pledges eternal loyalty . . ."

With one last breath, Fa-Ying hurled herself up the middle of the room, flinging herself in a prostrate ball at her father's feet. The room grew silent as the King looked down at her; then, amused, he scooped her up into his lap while motioning for the interpreter to continue.

". . . and who wishes to present his most beautiful daughter, Tuptim, for His Majesty's royal favor."

Absently, King Mongkut stroked his daughter's hair while gazing at the woman before him. She was most extraordinarily beautiful, though her composed features gave no hint of whatever emotions flared inside her—fear? awe? anticipation? rage? After a moment he nodded appreciatively. With a bow five of his courtiers stood and walked over to Tuptim, then without a word bore her away.

"Father," said Fa-Ying. She tugged imploringly at the sigil of office that hung around his neck. "Father—!"

He bent his head as she whispered quickly, then turned and looked down at her in amazement.

"Is this true?"

She nodded solemnly. Taking her by the hand,

King Mongkut stood. With a curt nod he dismissed his officials. Then, Fa-Ying in tow, he strode from the Audience Hall toward the Children's Garden.

"What has happened here?" he cried.

In front of the Golden Pavilion people clustered like so many feeding butterflies. Royal wives in gold and red, concubines in their long fluttering silks, and—squeezing between them all—the royal children, squealing and chattering with excitement. At the sound of the King's voice every one of them dropped to the ground—all save Fa-Ying, who still clutched her father's hand. Frowning, the King stepped over first one still form and then another, until he reached the door and could peer inside.

At the front of the room Anna Leonowens sat, calmly reading her Siamese primer. Behind her, Louis Leonowens stood before the chalkboard, laboriously filling it with the same sentence:

I WILL NOT FIGHT IN SCHOOL

I WILL NOT FIGHT IN SCHOOL

I WILL NOT FIGHT IN SCHOOL

Beside the other chalkboard, Prince Chulalongkorn sat defiantly and glared at the English boy. His servants stood behind him, at a loss as to how to handle this particular royal mishap. As King Mongkut stood surveying the room, Lady Thiang appeared at his shoulder.

"The British boy pushed Chulalongkorn, Your Majesty," she said in a low voice. At his desk, the Crown Prince lifted his chin triumphantly and smiled.

For a minute or two King Mongkut stood, brooding. His gaze flickered from his son to Louis, and once again he stared at the chalkboard.

I WILL NOT FIGHT IN SCHOOL

Most interesting, he thought, and looked at Anna curiously. But to Lady Thiang he only said, "Why?"

Several of the royal wives had crept in through the door and now stood watching the goings-on. Lady Thiang cast them a helpless glance, but as none of them spoke English, it was left to her to reply. She hesitated, reluctant to speak the truth. Finally she said haltingly, "Prince insult memory of boy's dead father."

King Mongkut remained a moment longer, staring measuringly at his son. Then, to the astonishment of everyone there—royal wives and concubines, tittering children, Lady Thiang, and Anna and Louis, but most of all Prince Chulalongkorn—without another word the King turned and walked away.

"You will finish writing your thousand sentences," Anna said with a nod to her son. "And you, Prince, will remain here until you have done the same."

It was twilight when Louis wrote the final sentence. His arm ached, his fingers felt as though they would never straighten, but—

"Nine hundred ninety-nine," he gasped, the chalk a mere nub in his hand, "one thousand. Finished."

His mother regarded him coolly. "Then you may go home."

"Aren't you coming?"

"Not until Prince Chulalongkorn has completed his task."

Louis nodded obediently, turned, and started for the door. Before reaching it he stopped. He looked back at Prince Chulalongkorn, still sitting defiantly with his retinue behind him, and in a quiet voice said, "My father was a hero."

Anna gazed with love and mild surprise at her son. To think he had such passion inside him, and such self-control! But Prince Chulalongkorn only gave the English boy a sullen stare and sank deeper into his seat. Anna sighed, watching him: the road to educating the future king of Siam was going to be a long and bumpy one.

Dusk deepened to night, and still the Prince did not move. Behind him his guards stood and occasionally drifted off to sleep, awakening with a start. Anna lit the candles, long white tapers that cast black shadows across the pavilion's petal-strewn floor, sat, and continued to read her primer. Outside, birds called drowsily back and forth, and once she heard the tiny *yowp* of a hunting gecko as it caught a moth in its fierce little jaws. But other than that the garden was silent: royal mothers and children had retreated to the Inner City, and when Beebe had poked her head in hours earlier, Anna had dismissed her gently.

"Thank you, Beebe, but I must wait until the Prince finishes his work."

Beebe's scowl told exactly what she thought of the Crown Prince, but she nodded to Anna and left quietly.

The first crickets were chirping, and bats slicing the violet sky, when a sound caused Anna to drop her book. Across the Children's Garden snaked a line of bobbing lanterns: servants, at least twenty of them, all bearing the makings of an elaborate supper. Lady Thiang was at the procession's head, and as they entered the pavilion, she gestured at the desks. The servants immediately began laying out bright silk tablecloths and setting down baskets and platters heaped with food: fruits carved like birds and flowers, bowls of steaming bird's-nest soup, rice with chilis and fish sauce, steamed fish, sticky rice balls rolled with tiny prawns, spicy salads and coconut custards and *dhal*. The air filled with the fragrance of coriander and chili, and the sweet, flowery scent of jasmine tea. Prince Chulalongkorn jumped to his feet, but before he could move, Anna intercepted Lady Thiang.

"I'm sorry, Lady Thiang, but this will have to wait. The Prince has not yet been dismissed."

Lady Thiang's eyes met hers, and for the first time Anna saw her not as a royal wife or concubine, but as a mother. "I understand," Lady Thiang replied, and dipped her head almost imperceptibly at the Prince. "His Majesty, King Mongkut, afraid schoolteacher might get hungry during long night ahead. He send food—for one."

Anna fought a smile—though she couldn't stop her mouth from watering. She *wai*ed graciously to Lady Thiang.

"Tell His Majesty I am most grateful for my supper."

At his desk, Prince Chulalongkorn stood, jaw dropping in amazement. Then, quick as thought, he raced to the blackboard and began frantically writing across it in Siamese. The two women traded a smile.

"I think," said Anna, "that I may need a little assistance in cleaning my plate."

Lady Thiang nodded. "Chulalongkorn help, I'm sure."

The candles had burned to mere stubs before the Crown Prince finished filling the chalkboard with his elegant, swooping penmanship. He sat beside Anna, wolfing down dinner as she gathered her books. When she turned to leave, he lifted his head and asked, "Why does my father humble me?"

Anna stopped and stared at him, seeing the genuine hurt and concern in the boy's eyes. "Because people do not see the world as it is, but as *they* are. A good king needs a broader view. Your father understands this, because during his years as a monk he lived in many places, and met many different kinds of people. You have only grown up in the palace, but you will learn, Your Highness."

Chulalongkorn sat thoughtfully, pondering her words. Anna smiled and started once more for the door. As she did, a soft breeze stirred through the pavilion and set the candle flames leaping. There was the burbling song of some nightbird, and then another, more disturbing sound—a low, mournful cry. Anna paused, trying to trace it to its source, then hurried into the garden.

"Stay here," she called to Prince Chulalongkorn.

The night was still, cooled by an intermittent breeze and the gently plashing fountains. Anna stood in the path, listening—and there it came again. She walked quickly away from the pavilion, and in a moment she determined that the sound came from outside the Children's Garden. She gave a brief glance back at the pavilion, but decided that the Prince would be safe there with his guards. Then she pushed open the heavy gates and stepped outside.

The grounds of the Grand Palace were a maze of streets and alleys and narrow canals, bounded by high walls and the carefully tended grounds of mansions and houses where the King's retainers and officials lived. Lights spilled from their windows, and occasionally a burst of laughter or conversation.

Still she could not find where that sorrowful voice was coming from. The low keening sound rose and fell but did not cease. As Anna followed it, she drew farther and farther from the palace's central precincts, and onto a street where she had not been before. There she found herself standing before an imposing mansion, its stone outer walls fringed with pale-bearded orchids. Anna frowned: could the crying possibly have come from here?

And then it sounded again—louder, and yes, if she craned her neck she could just make out a narrow passage at the side of the house, dark and dank beneath rain gutters and the heavy limbs of giant rhododendrons. She glanced around, saw no one, and quickly walked down the path.

It led into a narrow courtyard behind the house, a squalid place rank with weeds and heaps of rotting garbage. As she entered the courtyard another, even more putrid smell made her grimace. She withdrew a handkerchief and covered her mouth and nose with it, then stepped carefully around a mound of decaying fruit. Moonlight filtering through the leaves gave everything a sickly, pallid look, as though Anna were seeing it through a clouded glass. A few feet away something stirred, sending a small flurry of leaves down from an overhanging branch. Anna froze, looked up, and gasped.

In the center of the courtyard was a low stone trough. Chained to this was a woman, though it took a moment for Anna to understand that this *was* a woman. A shrunken, twisted figure, hair matted and naked torso dark with running sores, she was hunched over the trough, hopelessly scouring a chamber pot in the moonlight. Her lower body was caked with excrement and dried blood, and around one swollen, bloody ankle was an iron manacle, attached to a chain that stretched across the yard.

"What is that *smell*?"

Anna whirled to see Prince Chulalongkorn standing at the edge of the courtyard behind her, pinching his nostrils. He held a lantern and stared bemused into the darkness, but when he raised the lamp, his expression turned to horror.

"*Oh*—" He recoiled, his eyes locking with Anna's as he sought an answer to what was before them. "Mem—?" he asked.

But as Anna turned helplessly from the boy to the shackled woman, she realized that, for once, she had no answer at all.

It was late that night when King Mongkut's military advisers told him of the attack. They had gathered in his library, an extraordinary sorceror's hideaway filled with every imaginable instrument of science: alembics, telescopes, telegraph receivers, sextants, a working model of a steam engine, and any number of globes. A huge map of Siam hung from one wall—a strategic map, with no sign of King Mongkut's visage anywhere upon it. He had been out on the terrace, observing the heavens with his telescope; from his expression, it was evident he would much prefer to be there now. Instead he sat, hand cupping his chin, and listened as General Alak and Prince Chowfa told him of the slaughter at Bang Pli.

"Who would order such a massacre?" the King said quietly when his brother had finished.

"They were Burmese," said Prince Chowfa. He had not yet changed his clothes; his uniform was dusty and sweat-stained, his face worn from his travels.

"So you've said. But the puppet who leads Burma has British strings. Why would the imperialists use such tactics?"

General Alak shook his head. "Because a war with one's neighbors brings the British to the rescue."

King Mongkut ignored the general's sharp tone.

"Men like you, Alak," he said evenly, "were not built for so much peace and prosperity."

"Peace makes men soft, Your Majesty." Alak gestured at the map behind him. "The English define Burma as a 'British Protectorate.' Vietnam and Cambodia are known throughout the world as 'French Indochina.' What will they call Siam?"

The King listened thoughtfully. "But suppose we make them our friends?" he said at last. "Would that not destroy them as enemies?"

"Is that why you've brought English into the palace?" demanded Prince Chowfa.

It was a moment before the King replied. "She is a good teacher."

General Alak and Prince Chowfa traded looks. "These are dangerous times, Your Majesty," Alak said at last. "A foreigner's influence could be equally so."

The other ministers began talking all at once. King Mongkut listened in silence, looking up as an aide hurriedly entered the room and delivered a note to the Kralahome. The Prime Minister glanced at Mongkut, then at the note—a handwritten missive on plain white paper. With a frown the Kralahome read it, his expression registering amazement at the author's audacity.

"You will excuse me, Your Majesty," he said, and left.

The Kralahome found Anna Leonowens in his office, standing impatiently by the window and ignoring the entreaties of a servant to leave.

"Mem Leonowens," the Kralahome began sternly.

"It is unconscionable!" Anna cried, whirling to face him. Her cheeks were pale and her hair disheveled, but her eyes glittered dangerously as she strode forward to meet him. "She has been left outside for six weeks, all because she tried to buy her own freedom!"

The Kralahome drew himself up, deciding to try another tack. "Mem Leonowens," he said in a tone of exaggerated patience, "the Lady Jao Jom Manda Ung is daughter of very influential family—"

"And when that woman La-Ore offered her the money, her mistress accused her of ingratitude and chained her like an animal in the yard where the Prince and I found her last night!"

The Kralahome's face darkened. "Heir to throne must *never* get involved in issue of bond servant. This will resolve itself in time."

"Like my house?" Anna said sarcastically.

"You are learning."

Anna spun on her heel, muttering under her breath. "It is like talking to a *brick wall* . . ."

Overhearing her, the Kralahome sighed. "Sometimes the best way to win is to surrender."

"And sometimes," Anna replied, "it is *not*."

She stalked back out of his chambers, holding her skirts and glaring at any servant who dared look at her. Few did, but by the time she returned to her classroom in the pavilion, her fury had subsided somewhat. She found Louis at the front of the room conducting an impromptu geography session. A brand-new map of the world hung in place of the one of Siam, and Louis was using a bamboo pointer to indicate various nations as the children chanted in unison.

"China, Japan, India, France, England, United States . . ."

Lady Thiang stood and watched, beaming. At the far side of the room, Prince Chulalongkorn sat at his desk, surrounded by servants who fanned him patiently. His boyish face, so much like his father's, was stern, almost impassively so. But the dark eyes the Prince turned to Anna as she entered were haunted, and very much a child's. Suddenly he stood and marched across the front of the room. Louis's hand dropped. The children fell silent as Prince Chulalongkorn confronted Anna and spoke.

"I have been doing much thinking, Mem Teacher," he said, his voice respectful but loud. "On why some in this life are masters, like Lady Jao Jom Manda Ung, and why others are slaves."

For a moment Anna said nothing. The Kralahome's edict still echoed in her head. Across the room, Lady Thiang's eyes fixed on the teacher, waiting for her reply. At last Anna said, "That is something you will need to ask your father, Your Highness."

"But you are teacher," Prince Chulalongkorn countered. He opened his hands to her in a gesture at once commanding and imploring. "Please: teach."

Anna stood, thinking. Then she turned and walked to where several wooden crates formed a makeshift bookshelf. She began to sort through these, pulling out first one book and then another before finding the one she wanted. She crossed back to Prince Chulalongkorn and handed the volume to him.

"*Uncle Tom's Cabin*," he pronounced slowly, struggling with the words.

"That was written by an American named Harriet Beecher Stowe. She asked the same question you did, Your Highness. Perhaps you should read her book before we continue this discussion."

A sudden smile made the Prince's face look radiant, and not boyish at all. He bowed to Anna. "I shall read it at once, Mem," he said, and returned to his desk.

Anna nodded, then as Louis took up his pointer once more, she wandered over to the doorway. For some time she stood there, staring out at the Children's Garden, with its fountains and tame birds, its hibiscus and fruit trees. But her thoughts were in another, darker place, as her gaze dropped from the enchanted vista before her to the plain gold wedding band on her finger.

five

Within the Hidden City other hidden places nested, like scallop shells placed one inside another: all part of the secret, sacred domain of women, the homes and chambers of royal wives and beloved concubines; lovers who had fallen from favor, forgotten now and forced to dwell within echoing corridors where the other women would not meet their eyes; and newcomers striving for the attention of the man they must acknowledge as Lord of Life. An entire world within the world, with its own laws and torments, its own rituals and commonplace sorceries.

Yet within even the inmost heart of the Hidden City, still more hidden places existed, and it was to one of these that Tuptim was brought. She went

89

willingly, because she knew no other way; it would have been no use pleading that she was too young, too far from home, too much alone here among all these strange women. Because they had all been too young once, and far from home, and save for those who were sisters, or daughters, they had all been strangers, too.

So she let herself be led in silence to the chamber where she would await the King. Through twisting corridors and open gardens where the rarest orchids grew, flowers prized not only for their scent or color but for the human attributes they embodied: calanthe orchids like eyes, magenta grassland orchids thrusting out like eager tongues, phallic *denrobium unicum* and yellow Venus slipper, the tiny violet blossoms called children of the air, and the great blue Vanda orchid, which grew only in the uppermost mountain heights and here within the Hidden City, floating in carefully tended porcelain bowls. Tuptim nodded obediently when her handmaidens pointed these out, and the aviaries bright with bird song and fluttering parrots; but her eyes did not really see these wonders. The most beautiful daughter of Siam's most prosperous tea merchant was a hidden city unto herself, and within the deepest chamber of her heart she held the image of the young man who had run alongside her sedan chair in the streets of Bangkok, his voice echoing desolately above the cries of street vendors and begging children.

Balat. His name drummed inside her now; nothing would drown it out.

"Here, Lady Tuptim . . ."

It was Lady Thiang who spoke, her voice reassuring as she placed a hand upon Tuptim's neck and gently guided her through the last arched doorway. They had reached her room, the one Tuptim had not been permitted to see until this hour. A room swathed in shadow and half-light, its walls like the chambers of a heart, folds of crimson and indigo and scarlet silk and brocade. At one end a bed that was more like a raised stage for the *nang*, the shadow theater, all shimmering drapes and flickering with candle flame, droplets of light bouncing from small mirrors set into bedposts and sconces.

". . . come, Lady."

They brought her to the bed, where a raised dais of gilded teak glowed in the candlelight like an altar. At each end gleamed candles and brass lanterns; there was the heavy fragrance of incense, and those water hyacinths which smell of oranges. Tuptim sat cross-legged upon the dais and, extending her arms, let the women begin.

Piece by piece they removed her clothing, the long panels of jade-colored silk and the pearl-beaded jacket her mother had given her before she left home. From a hidden alcove someone struck the notes of a lyre, plangent, heartbreaking as the sound of the first rains. The women surrounded her, silent now and intent upon their part in the ritual. Lady Thiang loosed Tuptim's hair from its stiff topknot, let it fall in a long, straight sheaf to her breasts, and began to brush it, slowly, with the long-tined silver combs used only on this occasion. When she had finished, she combed civet into Tuptim's hair, dabbing her fingertips in a tiny lacquered container. The musk melted into the thick mass and made it shine as though oiled.

"Here, Lady."

They loved warm scented water from a silver basin and washed her, crushed the blossoms of night-blooming jasmine against her bare skin. Last of all, they dried her in a single length of silk some twenty feet long, then dressed her in a robe the pure deep yellow of Venus slippers, its sleeves embroidered with sacred words.

"You are trembling," said Lady Thiang softly. She gestured at the others, and they began to set out silver and lacquered bowls of fruit, melons and pineapples and guavas carved and arranged in suggestive patterns; *look coop*—miniature fruits of bean paste and sugar—glasses of sweetened coconut milk with petals of shaved ginger floating in them, and ornate betel-nut holders. "Do not fear, blessed one. His Majesty is a kind and generous lover."

Tuptim's eyes met Lady Thiang's. Her heart pounded so that she was afraid to speak, lest her lover's name fly out, but she nodded gratefully at the older woman. Lady Thiang laid her palm against Tuptim's cheek and smiled, then stood.

"Come," she said in an urgent whisper. A wash of golden lamplight spilled across the silken draperies: the King's retinue was approaching. Silently, each one stopping to *wai* deeply before her, Tuptim's entourage dispersed. There was a moment when she felt more completely alone than she ever had. Then the curtains hanging in front of the door stirred. The King stood there, wearing a robe identical to Tuptim's.

"Lord," she whispered, and prostrated herself before him. She could feel tears, fear, and the bitter fruit of the betrayal she held within her like a sickness, but then there was a hand upon her neck. Gently, as though lifting an infant, King Mongkut took her face in his hands and raised it. He was kneeling in front of her, his eyes kind but ardent, too, as he gazed at her in the candlelight. He leaned forward, drawing her to him, as Tuptim closed her eyes and tried to smile.

The hard spring rains lashed the city, sluicing away torrents of garbage, rotting fruit and fallen leaves, fish heads and feathers left from slaughter. In the mean back courtyard of Lady Jao Jom Manda Ung, the rain washed clean the trough where La-Ore had labored, and scoured the rusting chains and anklet which had once held her prisoner.

The rains fell on Anna's house as well, as she and Louis rushed around, frantically trying to ready themselves for school. On the front porch Moonshee waited with an umbrella. He stared calmly up at the gray-swept sky, handing the umbrella to Anna as she and her son clattered down the front steps.

"You have a visitor," he said, inclining his head.

Anna and Louis stopped dead in their tracks. In the middle of the walkway stood the Kralahome, followed by his entourage and a half dozen glowering Amazon guards bearing red umbrellas. Anna paled.

"Were you not commanded to leave slave issue alone?" thundered the Kralahome.

Without thinking, Anna touched the finger that had once worn her wedding band. "Your Excellency," she began. "I am fully prepared to obey His Majesty's commands within the obligation of my duty to his family, but beyond that I can promise no obedience."

The Kralahome stared at her coldly. "You will follow," he said, and began to walk away.

Anna hesitated, then started after him. Louis remained rooted to the bottom step.

"Mother?" he called, frightened.

"I have done nothing wrong, dear," said Anna, her voice steadier than she felt. "Go on with Moonshee."

She followed the Kralahome, dodging puddles and darting beneath pavilions for shelter when she could. At last they reached the Audience Hall. Rain slashed at the open windows and echoed loudly from the tiled roof, and beneath Anna's shoes the floor felt slick and treacherous. Through the long side window she could see the palace's ornamental lake, stirred to muddy froth by the storm.

At the front of the hall King Mongkut sat upon his throne, regarding the imposing figure of the dowager Lady Jao Jom Manda Ung where she knelt, fuming, before him. She was a hard-eyed woman in late middle age, loved neither by her servants nor her own family. Mongkut had no doubt but that, had the heavens allowed, she would treat the King with no more courtesy than she did her slaves. Beside her, a half dozen slaves fanned her frantically, trying to bring her temper down as she self-consciously twisted the simple gold ring on her finger.

"She tricked me! She broke into my own home, set my servant free, then came to me with an offer to buy her and made payment!"

King Mongkut slid his reading glasses onto his nose and looked back down at the copy of the Slave Laws the Kralahome had given him that morning. A sudden stir at the back of the room made him glance. There was Anna, head held high as she strode into the hall with the Kralahome close behind.

"La-Ore purchased her freedom once, Your Majesty." The Englishwoman's voice rang out clearly above the sound of the rain. She did not see

Prince Chulalongkorn, standing off by himself behind a pillar and watching her in silence. "I believe had I given this woman my ring first, she would have kept it and continued to hold La-Ore captive."

Lady Jao Jom Manda Ung glared at her as King Mongkut eyed them both wearily.

"King's commitment to noble families must not be compromised," he said, holding up the Slave Laws.

"Your Majesty—"

Anna took a deep breath, then continued. "In your letter confirming my employment, you claimed you wanted Siam to take its place among the nations of the modern world. You spoke of 'building something greater' than yourself—'a country where no man is above the law.' Which is why I chose to come here."

She fell silent. King Mongkut studied her, and under his fierce gaze Anna looked away, embarrassed and, yes, perplexed by what she had—most uncustomarily—revealed about the real reason she'd journeyed to Siam.

Finally: "Schoolteacher has outstanding memory," said the King.

This was too much for Lady Jao Jom Manga Ung. She began haranguing His Majesty, shaking the finger that now wore Anna's wedding ring.

"I want my slave returned—immediately! And punishment of this insolent English who dares to *stand* before the Lord of Life!"

Behind his pillar, Prince Chulalongkorn shifted, angling himself so that he could see both his father and Mem Leonowens. King Mongkut rubbed his chin thoughtfully, eying the Kralahome where he waited beside Anna. It was several minutes before the King spoke.

"Kralahome, if you would please honor the Lady Jao Jom with an explanation of the law."

The Kralahome turned to the dowager and bowed. "Regretfully, Lady Jao Jom Manga Ung, I must inform you that bond servants have the right, by law, to buy their own freedom." He picked up a scroll on an adjoining table, opened it, and read aloud from the statutes regarding slavery.

"And what if every slave in my service should bring me the price of their freedom?" Lady Jao Jom's voice rose to a shriek when he finished. "Am I bound to serve myself?"

The King smiled at her graciously. "That would

be most unfortunate, my august mistress."

With a furious cry Lady Jao Jom got to her feet. She shot Anna a piercing look, then with a grand gesture tore Anna's wedding ring from her hand, marched to the window, and hurled it out. For an instant it hung in the steely air like another raindrop; then the ring dropped and disappeared into the depths of the lake. Without a word, Lady Jao Jom Manga Ung turned and stormed out, slaves trailing her as the fascinated Prince Chulalongkorn watched furtively from his hiding place.

For a long moment the Great Hall was silent. Yet to Anna it did not seem that she stood there, surrounded by courtiers and slaves, but in a quieter place, where a cool Sussex rain beat against the little windows of a stone chapel, and the smells of roses and peonies rose from the small bouquet she clutched. She blinked, feeling tears, and stared at the gray folds of her silken dress.

And the King stared at her, puzzled, almost angered, by her sacrifice and his own inability to fully understand it—or her.

"Why did you intervene?" he said at last.

"Because my conscience demanded it."

"And boys' fisticuffs?"

"I beg your pardon?"

The King gave her a condescending look. "I suppose since you must be both mother and father to son, tendency to overprotect is strong."

"Louis can take care of himself, Your Majesty," said Anna tartly. "It was your son I was protecting. But thank you for the dinner"—she curtsied and turned to go—"although I don't think it was necessary."

"I know my son. You would still be there."

Anna stopped. "Perhaps," she said, eyes flashing. "But *my* point would have been made. Not yours."

King Mongkut tapped his chin. "Husband must have been very understanding."

Anna drew herself to her full height and stared fearlessly up at the throne. "My husband was never threatened by my ideas and opinions."

The King met the challenge in her gaze with his own, and waited for her to look away.

She did not. A full minute passed before he said, "And because I am also such a man, I will allow you to always stand upright in my presence. Providing head shall never be higher than mine."

Anna curtsied gracefully. "Thank you, Your

Majesty." She stole a look at the Kralahome. He was staring at her in disbelief, his face red. It was unheard of, that anyone could stand taller than a member of the royal family! Then, with a rustle of taffeta and crinoline, Anna turned and walked out of the Audience Hall.

"Too many buttons," murmured the King as he watched her go.

The Kralahome shook his head. "Your Majesty, I believe there has been enough insult caused by this woman who believes herself to be the equal of a man."

"Not the equal of a man, Chao Phya," said the King. His gaze remained fixed on the door. "The equal of a king."

Anna found her students sitting obediently at their desks, spellers open before them, hands neatly clasped. But their faces revealed that they, too, knew exactly where she had been, and why. Anna kept her own face calm and strode purposefully to her desk. Before she could sit, however, a white-clad figure came bounding up the aisle to set a picture before her.

"I make this for you tomorrow!" Fa-Ying piped proudly.

Anna smiled. "Why, thank you, Fa-Ying! It's beautiful."

The little girl pointed at the page, all green inky blots and carefully drawn stick figures colored in red and blue. "These are monkeys at Summer Palace."

"This must be your father." Anna pointed at a tiny figure next to the King. "And this must be you."

Fa-Ying nodded in delight. Anna stooped and gave her a hug. "I shall hang it on my wall at home."

"I will make another for you yesterday!"

"Then I will wait for it tomorrow."

Fa-Ying skipped back to her desk. Smiling after her, Anna slipped the drawing into her bag. When she looked up, she saw Lady Thiang approaching. Beside her was a slender young woman in blue silk, her hair beautifully coiffed but her face pale. She no longer wore her lavish finery, but Anna recognized the ethereal woman she had glimpsed in the palanquin several days before.

"Good morning, Lady Thiang," Anna said. "How are you today?"

"I am well, Mem Leonowens, thank you. This is Lady Tuptim, sir. She is new to palace also like yourself, but have no son to keep her company."

"Hello, Lady Tuptim," said Anna. "My name is Anna."

"I wish also to learn writing of English, Mem," Tuptim replied awkwardly. "To please His Majesty, King Mongkut."

Anna stared at the young woman with curiosity. Tuptim's empty gaze belied her words. The Englishwoman measured her own before saying, "Of course. But I should hope it would please Lady Tuptim as well."

She bent over her desk and found an English primer, handed it to Tuptim. The young woman took the book gratefully and gave Anna a small smile.

"We all have much to learn from each other, I think," said Anna. Tuptim bowed and stepped away. Lady Thiang remained a moment longer, her eyes warm.

"That is so, sir," she agreed, and turning, she escorted Tuptim back to the Hidden City.

In the weeks that followed, all of Anna's students began to learn, and as she had predicted, their lessons were varied. Every Monday morning she would walk to the front of the room and modify the writing on the chalkboard. LETTER OF THE WEEK: E gave way to LETTER OF THE WEEK: F, and then G, and H, until one day Anna was shocked to realize that they were halfway through the alphabet.

But her charges were not just learning their letters. One afternoon when the children had been dismissed early, Anna took a stroll around the royal lake, closing her eyes as she lifted her face to the sun and breathing happily the mingled scents of roses and sun-warmed water.

This, at least, is not much different from summer in England, she thought.

"You've got him!"

The excited cry made her open her eyes and scan the lake. There on the shore beneath the King's royal study, she spied Louis and Prince Chulalongkorn, up to their knees and soaked to the skin, the Prince triumphantly holding up a very large frog.

And this, too, is as it should be.

Anna beamed, raising her hand and waving at the boys. She did not see the flash of light in the window of the royal study above them. If she had, she might have traced it to the eye of King Mongkut's telescope, and perhaps have glimpsed the man behind the instrument, spectacles pushed close against his face as he gazed down at the playing boys. His expression mirrored Anna's, delight and pride in equal measure, but when he saw the flutter of her pale blue dress in the breeze, he turned his instrument slightly to focus on her. His expression changed then, and it might have been just as well that Anna could not see the tenderness that took the place of pride, or the more complicated wash of emotions that the King himself was having some difficulty naming.

Others were learning, too. Every morning Lady Tuptim showed up for class with the children, taking her place at the back of the room. For all her promptness in arriving each day, and the serious expression she affected as Anna read excerpts from Shakespeare and Keats and Dickens, still the teacher suspected that Tuptim was not quite as focused upon her studies as she appeared. In the afternoons Tuptim and the older children practiced their penmanship, filling long sheets of yellow paper with carefully shaped block letters. Yet the name that Tuptim copied painstakingly upon her page was not her own, but one that Anna did not recognize—*Balat*—written over and over and over, as though it were a charm or talisman.

Anna pretended not to notice. She was more grat-ified to see Prince Chulalongkorn in the pavilion, long after the others had gone off to fly kites or splash in the lake, sitting and reading *Uncle Tom's Cabin* while his loyal retinue patiently fanned him. She knew better than to comment on the Prince's initiative. Instead she inspected the little menagerie the children had assembled. They all seemed to have inherited their father's passion for science, and delighted in capturing small creatures in the royal city's gardens and then transferring their captives to the series of vivariums that now lined the back of the classroom. Large glass bowls, at Anna's request labeled with both their English and Latin names in various examples of childish handwriting—

TIMBER BEETLE *Eurybatus ferrouses*
GOLDEN ORB WEAVER *Nephila maculata*
CROCODILE SALAMANDER *Tylototrition verrucosus*

The *chingcoks* and *tokkaes*, the house geckos, were not imprisoned; she stopped to watch one crawling across the ceiling as it stalked a mosquito. Some of them were tame enough to eat insects from your fingers. That afternoon she had watched with interest as Fa-Ying fed one a caterpillar, the little girl uncharacteristically still as the emerald lizard crept across her palm. As any good teacher would, Anna tried very hard not to play favorites with her students, but it was hard not to fall under the tiny princess's spell. She was bright and indefatigably energetic, exhausting even her older siblings in their complicated games of tag and beetle hunting, but she also loved to clamber into Anna's lap, sometimes falling asleep there in the heat of the long tropical afternoons. King Mongkut was often a stern figure to his children, but Anna had never seen him be anything but the gentlest of fathers to Fa-Ying. Lady Thiang had confided in her that the child was Mongkut's favorite. Her mother, who had been his queen, had died only two years earlier; Prince Chulalongkorn was her full brother. Fa-Ying accompanied her father on royal processions and interviews where not even his ministers could gain entry; she sat curled in his lap during diplomatic meetings, sleepy and silent as a loris, and sat next to him during meals.

And she accompanied her father when he awaited Anna the next morning on the royal gondola—the

Suphanahongsa, or *Golden Hansa*, an immense high-prowed ship that was like something from a dream. Anna drew in her breath sharply when she saw it, and Louis cried out loud in delight.

"Mother! It's a *dragon* ship!"

Anna thought it looked more like a cross between a dragon and a swan, the creature's soaring head and neck of gilded teakwood with alabaster eyes, and ornamented with huge looping wreaths of hibiscus and frangipani. "It is the sacred mount that Brahma rides upon," King Mongkut explained as he helped his bedazzled guests on board. "Fifty men must row it. This is not full procession, of course— that would be fifty-one barges and three thousand men," he said, eyes twinkling as he noted Anna's amazement.

"Goodness!" she said, steadying herself alongside a low, cushioned seat. She did not notice her luggage piled on the enormous deck above them. "It is *quite* extraordinary, Your Majesty."

"It is indeed," said King Mongkut. He crossed his arms and stood behind the prow, gazing with pride at the gold-washed canal surrounding them. Fa-Ying stood nearby in the same pose, a tiny feminine reflection of her father. Beside her the Kralahome stood sullenly, overseeing an attendant preparing betel trays for the King. "It is indeed."

Three smaller escort gondolas, *rua saeng*, darted out from the shore, glinting green in the sunlight. With a shout the oarsmen began to row, chanting as the *Golden Hansa* started to slide across the smooth water. It took only minutes for them to travel from the canal to the wider, amber-colored expanse of the river, joining the traffic there of canoes and fishing boats whose captains called out to one another excitedly as the royal procession approached.

"The Chao Phraya River is lifeline to the most fertile valley in all of Asia," King Mongkut announced. He gestured at the river loftily, as though he himself had created it.

And indeed he might have, to judge from the reaction of the townspeople crowding its banks. Anna watched in amazement as seemingly all of Bangkok rushed to the water's edge, prostrating themselves before the King.

"Capital moved here to this site after fall of our first great capital, Ayudhya, one hundred years ago. Burmese king set siege to old capital and took thirty thousand of our people prisoner. So we moved capital here."

Anna stood and gazed at the scene passing before her. The prostrate commoners, and behind them thickets of lush greenery where macaques swung from the trees and kingfishers swooped; the floating houses and *sala*, open pavilions, where elders sat placidly watching the river traffic; the gorgeous, soaring spires of *wats* with their lily-flower capitals—built, the King explained, in homage to the great lost glory of the ancient city of Ayudhya.

It moved Anna strangely: the cloying heat, the riverbank architecture strange and suggestive as orchid blossoms, the smells of decaying fish and vegetables fighting above the fragrance of jasmine water sprinkled over the deck by the King's attendants. She blinked, drawing a hand to her cheek and staring dreamily at the river. A few feet away, Louis did the same.

"Your boy is most appreciative of my kingdom's beauty," the King said.

"How could he not be, Your Majesty? It's extraordinary . . . and most humbling."

The King smiled in approval, regarding her with intense interest. He had dressed with especial care that morning, telling himself that it was because of the meeting he would have with the bishop that afternoon. He absently smoothed the front of his crimson silk blouson, eyes narrowing as he turned and tried to view his kingdom as Anna Leonowens did.

"Your people are very happy to see you." Anna inclined her head toward the riverbank, and Louis waved at the throngs rushing to prostrate themselves at the water's edge.

"It is matter of regret that King cannot be among them more." He turned to where his little daughter was herself waving, and gave her a squeeze. "*Looja* loves the river . . ."

Fa-Ying nodded shyly and gazed up at her father with adoring eyes.

Anna smiled. "She told me all about her journey to Ayudhya, and said it was the center of the universe."

"Yes. It is home to Ancient Ones and their many legends."

"I told her that in England we have Camelot."

Fa-Ying nodded eagerly. "And they had a big round table!"

"Everyone should have legends, I think." Anna reached down to stroke the child's hair. "They allow us to dream."

111

The King regarded her thoughtfully. "You are interesting mix of fact and fancy, Mem."

"I suppose it's because I surround myself with children." Anna's voice was strained, and she turned to stare down at the water. "I—I didn't have a choice, really."

The King nodded. "Buddhists believe all life is suffering. To take away pain of husband's death takes away Mem's chance to grow."

"We might have preferred a different lesson."

"Yes, but unique opportunity to change world would have passed to someone else."

Anna turned, surprised at the King's tone. He was staring directly at her, with the same fervor he had moments before focused upon his people on the riverbank. Uneasy, she looked away and called out to her son. "Louis, darling—do try and stay in the boat."

She hesitated, then turned back to the King. His gaze remained fixed on Anna, his dark eyes bright, almost questioning. Despite his avid look, Anna found herself unable to glance away. She swallowed, finally said, "Yesterday he asked about your flag and the white elephant, and I didn't have an answer."

112

The King drew himself up. "Louis Leonowens!" he commanded.

Reluctantly, Louis tore himself away from watching the oarsmen. He stood before the King, slightly fearful. "Yes, Your Majesty?"

King Mongkut smiled at Anna. "*I* am teacher now."

He pointed to where the Siamese flag billowed in the breeze high overhead. "The flag of Siam. Red is for . . ."

"Courage!" cried Fa-Ying.

The King nodded approvingly. "White . . ."

"Compassion!"

The King raised a finger at Louis. "The white elephant is Siam's most rare and honored creature." He turned to his daughter and said, "Perhaps on journey to Rice Festival, we will all see one."

"Rice Festival?" said Anna.

With a cry Louis suddenly lunged forward, nearly plunging off the side of the boat. "Mother! *Look!*"

Anna stood, shading her eyes, and felt as though the world were tilting around her. Before them the river narrowed and twisted beneath overhanging trees heavy with white blossoms. Extending into the waterway was a wide dock, strewn with white and pink

113

petals, and at the end of this stood Moonshee and Beebe, waving joyously. Behind them, tucked into a grove of rhododendrons, was a beautiful two-story house, in the Siamese style but built of faded rose-colored brick. Servants scurried in and out of its doors, already unpacking baskets full of Anna's things.

"Your Majesty," she said, her eyes brimming. "I believe you've finally rendered me speechless."

"I trust you will find ample space for engaging in English traditions," said King Mongkut. "Even for growing of roses."

He smiled, and for once there was no hint of hauteur in his face, just a delight as keen as Anna's own.

"Oh!" she cried, racing to stand beside Louis as the gondola pulled up to the dock. "It's *lovely*!"

The King beamed as his attendants hurried to help them onshore. Fa-Ying ran ahead, laughing and pointing things out to Louis—flowers, a butterfly, a tiny spirit house nearly overgrown by vines. Only when they stood in the little river-fronted garden did Anna turn and ask Mongkut coyly, "However, I am very curious. Is this because of our agreement, or are you simply trying to get rid of me?"

The King gazed up at the blazing blue sky, then at Anna.

"Yes," he said enigmatically.

"Come on, Mother!" Louis yelled impatiently from the front steps. Laughing, Anna lifted her skirts and hurried to join him. Moonshee and Beebe greeted her gaily, Moonshee pointing at the broad second-floor veranda as Anna stopped to admire a pretty canopy of fig vines near the door.

"A little soap and water, and we will have a fine house, Mem," he announced with pride.

"Shall I make us some tea?" called Beebe.

"That would be lovely." Anna glanced back at the King, standing with his daughter on the riverbank. She raised her hand to him and smiled. The King nodded in return, then headed back to the gondola.

"I like it when she smiles," said Fa-Ying as they climbed back on board.

"Yes, my darling," the King replied. He stood beside her, his hand absently caressing her head. His gaze was still fixed upon the slender woman in pearl gray taffeta, waving from the steps of her new home. The coxswain shouted to the crew. With an answering cry their oars dipped into the water, and the *Golden Hansa* began to make its way back to the palace. "I know . . . so do I."

six

It was another late evening for Mycroft Kincaid, a portly trader in his fifties whose ruddy face betrayed more exposure to claret and fine Tokay than it did to the sun. He walked unsteadily down the stone steps of the old rajah's plantation, and wished he'd spent a little more time learning about his host's gambling habits. The business venture that had spurred the night's visit had gone badly. And to make matters worse, he'd lost quite a bit more than he'd intended when he accepted the invitation to dinner.

Still, he comforted himself with the thought that he could win it all back tomorrow, if he wanted. These Siamese were notorious gamblers, betting on everything from kite combat to stag-beetle fights to where a leaf would fall upon the ground. One only had to raise a finger, and a wager could be made anywhere between Bangkok and the Burmese border.

"Damned stupid," he muttered, catching himself as he stumbled on a loose bit of mortar.

At the bottom of the steps he stopped, catching his breath, then looked up curiously. He could hear voices nearby, two men arguing, but his mastery of Siamese wasn't advanced enough to permit him to translate.

Probably more gambling, he thought, and headed to where his servants waited with his sedan chair.

Kincaid was wrong. A few yards away, hidden by the dense underbrush, a scar-faced man and a band of mercenaries waited, watching the shadows of the house's occupants as they moved across an upstairs window. The scar-faced leader inhaled deeply from his cheroot, sinking back on his haunches and fingering the handle of a dagger.

"What are we waiting for?" hissed one of the soldiers.

Their leader yanked his head, indicating Kincaid. "The English must not be harmed."

A few feet from his sedan chair, Kincaid paused. He took a few steps toward the forest, unbuttoned his fly, and began to relieve himself. Suddenly he stopped.

Something glowed in the darkness, not three yards away from him, a bright red ember that was neither firefly nor star. The breeze shifted, bringing with it the rank smell of a burning cheroot. Unnerved, Kincaid hastily buttoned himself and fled to his sedan chair. His servants carried him off. Moments later, a swarm of shadows emerged from the forest and descended upon the house, and the night cries of insects and birds were silenced by panicked screams.

The morning of the Rice Festival dawned clear and cool, a good augury for rain, but it was late afternoon before the royal procession was ready to depart. All day a flurry of activity filled the Grand Palace as wives and concubines, servants and children, bustled about, busying themselves with all the intense preparation for the journey. A half dozen servants bearing out the larger trunks passed where Anna sat watching it all, bemused.

"I would imagine that any time the whole family travels, it's quite an event," she said, thinking of what the word *family* defined in this instance—several hundred people and an entire herd of elephants.

"What exactly does one *wear* to a rice festival?"

Tuptim turned and held up a beautifully batiked, peacock blue sarong, a bit of cloth barely long enough to cover Anna's head.

"Oh, my." Anna bit her lip. "Well. Perhaps I'll have to dig through my trunk. Now if I can just find Louis . . ."

Tuptim folded her sarong and began plaiting her long black hair. "I remember first rice festival. Father took me as girl. People come from everywhere to see King. He bless all crops and it begin to rain. I think he was a god."

"And now?"

"He is also a man."

Anna nodded, the meaning behind Tuptim's words quite clear. "Well, I feel very fortunate indeed that we're invited."

"One cannot see Siam's beauty living in Bangkok, Mem. The mountains are so green, and the skies are more blue than your eyes."

Anna smiled, and Tuptim watched as she crossed the room to a window. A thoughtful, almost reluctant look passed across the royal concubine's delicate features as she stared at the sarong lying beside her purse and the basket containing her things for the festival. Finally she leaned down and extracted a letter from the purse.

"May I ask favor, Mem, to send this?"

Anna eyed the envelope curiously. Tuptim hesitated, then said, "I wish family to know how happy I am here with King."

Anna nodded. "When I was six years old, my parents sailed to India and left me behind to be educated in England. I didn't see them again for eight years. I know how consuming that ache can be— missing someone . . ."

She smiled ruefully, then took the letter. "I will have Moonshee find a messenger straight away."

"Thank you."

Anna walked to the window and stared outside. The late afternoon light tinged her hair with gold, and her cheeks were rosy from the day's sun. But the pale blue-gray eyes that gazed out upon the palace courtyard were sad. The younger woman waited, then gently asked, "How did husband die?"

"In my arms, actually." Anna's voice grew tight and she blinked, trying to focus on the serrated roof line of the neighboring *wat*. "Illness. Many of his regiment suffered the same fate."

"How did Mem survive?"

Anna turned. Behind her Tuptim stood, eyes brimming, hands hanging limply at her side. For all her beauty and the splendor of her surroundings, she looked very sad, and very, very young.

"The same way you will." Anna reached to touch the girl's hand. She smiled reassuringly. "One awful day at a time."

When it finally got underway, the royal procession of the summer Rice Festival was over a half mile long. And it seemed to Anna that with each swaying, lurching step of the elephant beneath her, they picked up still more people. Peasants mostly, running from their stilt-legged homes to shout and wave at the long, wavering line of elephants and horses, wagons and handcarts, royal wives and concubines, nobles of the inner court, flag bearers, elephant handlers, servants carrying parasols and an entire small army of cooks and kitchen staff. King Mongkut rode at the front of the long parade, seated in his royal *howdah* upon a bull elephant caparisoned with banners and wreaths of flowers. The King was reading a book and smoking a cheroot, seemingly oblivious to the sound of orchestral gongs and the piping of bamboo *khang*. Behind him, Anna rode with her son and the royal entourage, including Lady Thiang and the reserved Tuptim, all of them seated high above the ground in a magnificent wagon borne by four elephants.

"*Mem-sha!*" Fa-Ying scrambled, laughing, to plump herself into Anna's lap. "Louis teasing me! He say in England, coldness fall from sky like tiny feathers."

"Why would I lie about snow?" said the perplexed Louis, steadying himself as he sat beside his mother.

Fa-Ying let her head fall back as she stared up at the canopy of trees, bright sparks of sky flashing between the leaves. "Please, Mem, it is too hot. Can you make some now?"

Anna smiled. She smoothed strands of sweat-dampened hair from the child's brow and said, "Oh, Fa-Ying! Just because your father can make it rain doesn't mean I can make it snow."

"At last I discover her limitations."

Anna whirled to find herself eye-to=eye with the King on his royal elephant. She bowed respectfully and adopted a more formal tone. "I have many, Your Majesty."

"Father, will you make it snow?" pleaded Fa-Ying. "Please?"

King Mongkut looked fondly at his daughter. "Even for you, *looja*, I cannot. But I have seen photographs of such phenomenon. Blankets of it," he said, raising his hand to his chest. "Up to here."

He smiled and pulled another cheroot from his pocket, held it up for Louis.

"Smoke, Louis?"

Louis stared at him, eyes bulging. "Me? Jolly good!"

The King passed the cigar to an attendant. Louis reached over the rail of the swaying wagon, but before he could take the proffered smoke, his mother grabbed his belt and pulled him back in.

"But, Mother—he's the king! And—and Father smoked, too!"

Anna shook her head. "Your father was a man who had already achieved his full height."

"I have been smoking since age six, and some believe me to be giant among men," the King said solemnly.

Anna looked at him suspiciously. Could the King actually be *joking*? "A giant in intelligence as well as stature, Your Majesty," she said, and glanced at her son. "Which is why, Louis, I'm certain the King is pulling your leg."

Left: All heads turn admiringly to Anna as she sweeps in late to the anniversary dinner. The King compliments her, "Mem, you arrange all this to influence positive future of Siam and now you steal attention away from it."

Above: Princess Fa-Ying, the King's favorite daughter, melts hearts as she gives her father a big squeeze and kiss good night.

Below: "I have never danced with an Englishwoman before, Mem." "Nor I with a King."

General Alak and Prince Chowfa lead a small regiment of mounted and ground troops and cannon-mounted elephants toward a Burmese guerrilla camp.

"Khun Jao Tuptim, you are accused of a traitorous act against His Majesty, King Mongkut, which carries the penalty of death."

Left: King Mongkut, surrounded by his fifty-eight children, prays before a giant stone Buddha.

Below: The King feels a "chill come over him as if someone had just stepped on his grave" when he spots five hundred soldiers heading toward the royal family.

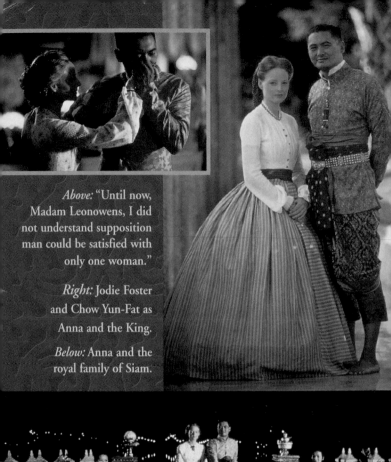

Above: "Until now, Madam Leonowens, I did not understand supposition man could be satisfied with only one woman."

Right: Jodie Foster and Chow Yun-Fat as Anna and the King.

Below: Anna and the royal family of Siam.

She turned back to the King. Recognizing the insistent glint in her eyes, he winked at Louis and pocketed the unlit cigar. Then he pointed, first at the boy, then Fa-Ying. "Now, I believe this is good time for all children to spread amazing concept of snow to cool off court, yes?"

"Yes, Father!" cried Fa-Ying. She wriggled from Anna's lap and ran to the back of the wagon. Louis followed her, and the adults were left alone.

"I simply meant to open conversation in controversial fashion Mem is so fond of," the King said innocently.

Anna looked up, unsure whether to take him seriously or not. "I do have my opinions . . . but they are merely that."

She gave him a small smile, but the King didn't respond, only continued to stare at her with rapt attention. Abashed by his gaze, Anna turned to gaze at the panoply of the forest around them, the tall tropical oaks and palms, alive with the cries of storks and pheasants and the bejeweled wings of dragonflies, all stirred by the procession. A minute passed before the King spoke again.

"Mem, I wish to compliment you for enlightening children to open minds and taste life. However, at this time I shall not offer cigar to your son, and you shall not teach this book to mine."

He held up the volume he had been reading: the copy of *Uncle Tom's Cabin* she had given to Chulalongkorn. Anna looked at him, not entirely surprised, as he continued. "Chulalongkorn has many questions, but one cannot plow fields overnight . . . even when soil is ripe to do so."

"I understand," said Anna in a low voice. She turned as a burst of laughter echoed from the rear of the wagon. There, standing on a platform before the giggling audience of her siblings, Princess Fa-Ying was miming a blanket of cold covering her thin shoulders.

"Today, however," pronounced the King, his eyes twinkling as he gestured at his daughter, "the challenge is—

"Snow!"

They reached the *wat*, the great temple, at dusk. Its base was formed of innumerable buttresses of pale marble, in the shape of the sacred white elephant, and from this the *wat* rose in row upon row of broad marble steps, each covered with offerings of fruits and flowers, sheaves of rice, and necklaces of wild orchids. Its central *prang* towered hundreds of feet above them, and four stairways, representing the four cardinal points, led to its summit. Coming upon it as they did, after hours of travel through the twilit jungle wilderness, was like discovering the sun ablaze in the middle of the night.

But they were not alone at the Altar of the Infinite—far from it. Thousands of worshipers had gathered at the foot of the temple, some of them after traveling for days from their remote northern villages. Around them the forest opened onto gently rolling green hills, stepped with ancient rice paddies and settlements. The villagers lay prostrate upon the ground, as high above them their Lord of Life knelt in prayer, uttering sacred invocations while hundreds of saffron-robed monks rang holy bells in concert.

In the shadow of a palm grove Anna stood with Louis at her side, watching silently. It was an extraordinary spectacle: the benevolent expressions of the nobles observing their ruler; the genuine love and respect shining from the faces of the peasants, their hand-hewn tools lying alongside them to be blessed; the utter peace and harmony of the world which King Mongkut was fighting to preserve. The vision of his world filled her, and she extended her hand to clasp her son's, the two of them united, and honored, by what lay before them.

Twilight deepened to night before the King's rituals of offering were completed. There was feasting then, the peasants occupying their own immense quadrant of the temple grounds, the King's entourage sitting around long tables piled high with extravagant dishes of fruits and salads, roasted fowl and steaming platters of fish. Afterward, they rejoined the thousands of villagers who waited expectantly at the foot of the temple, their voices high-pitched with excitement at what was to come.

"What is it?" whispered Anna to Lady Thiang. They sat upon benches piled high with cushions and embroidered silk blankets to ward off the nighttime chill. Overhead a canopy of stars blazed, as though they, too, honored the Lord of Life. King Mongkut sat directly behind Anna, flanked by the Kralahome and his attendants.

"It is *khon*—sacred play," Lady Thiang whispered back. "This is King's private troupe—actors have trained since childhood to wear masks of gods and demons here for great festival."

On the steps of the *wat* before them a proscenium

had been raised, tall carved pillars of teak wrapped round about with heavy brocade and banners that snapped in the breeze. Suddenly the sound of a gong echoed across the temple grounds. The vast crowd fell silent, save for the excited squeals of children—Fa-Ying and Louis among them. From the shadows emerged a group of figures clad in fabulous costumes thick with jewels and gilt. Their steps were mannered yet exquisitely graceful, their heads hidden by carved wooden masks as fantastic as the spires of the temple that reared above them—wonderful masks, depicting demons and gods, the monkey lord Hanuman and the great Aytuthadan King Phra Ram; his consort, Nang Sida; and numerous serpents and dragons, monstrous villains and mincing princesses. The air filled with clangs and pipes as the King's orchestra, the *piphat*, began to play in accompaniment to the drama. Lady Thiang leaned over and translated for Anna.

"Many years ago, when sickness and death were unknown to blessed people of Ayudhya, there was no Moon in sky, and Supreme Sun never withdrew bright face, even at night . . ."

The masked actors performed a stylized dance, arms tracing elaborate arabesques in the light of a thousand torches as they moved across the stage.

"So it was for a thousand years, until stars, angry at being dimmed by Sun's great light, schemed to stop his journey through sky by stealing his golden chariot."

The actors mimed rage and suspicion, and a small group broke away to form a line of scheming stars, their headdresses gleaming silver in the torchlight.

"But when they hid behind rainbow, waiting for thieving moment, Sun suddenly catch sight of sweet, pure, beautiful Princess of Ayudhya."

The actors froze. There was a crescendo of rippling notes upon the *ranad ek*, the great Siamese xylophone that was the heart of the orchestra, and the actors parted to reveal a tall woman in regal headdress, her face painted dead white, her eyes two long black-rimmed tears within an unearthly, beautiful face.

"And Sun's heart filled with rapture! He fly down and declared vows of eternal love."

Anna leaned forward, entranced. Behind her Prince Chulalongkorn pretended intense interest in the play, even as his hand reached delicately into his father's pocket to remove an uncut cigar.

"However," Lady Thiang continued, "while Sun

thus distracted, vengeful stars steal chariot."

The masked Sun and his shimmering Princess stood gazing into each other's eyes, while round about them the actors playing the scheming stars tiptoed, stealing his chariot. A ripple of delighted laughter swept the crowd as children giggled and called out to warn the oblivious lovers. Anna smiled; then, hearing a rustling in the shadows, she turned to see the King gazing at her, his own eyes as bewitched as those of the ensorceled Sun.

"When Sun learn of theft, all joy depart and large tears fall, as he could not now conduct bride to celestial kingdom."

The Sun unleashed a flood of tears. Unseen by anyone, Tuptim drew her hand to her cheek as a single tear fell there.

"And worse"—Lady Thiang's voice rose dramatically—"knowing all life dependent on him, noble Sun realized he must return to heavens. So he summon all strength at hand to will himself home, and bid farewell to his Princess."

With a heartbreaking gesture of farewell, the Sun parted from the stage. Abruptly all torches were extinguished. The assembled throng grew deathly quiet.

"That's it?" Anna whispered. "That's the end?"

Behind her, the King leaned forward, until she could feel the warmth of his breath upon her cheek. "Patience . . ." he murmured.

Onstage, a single lantern glowed, its wan light touching the glittering costumes of the stars as they ran back on. King Mongkut's low voice recited in Anna's ear. "But as clouds of sadness shrouded Sun and universe grew cold, regretful stars returned golden chariot. Sun, bright with happiness, shined with such great power he transformed bride into silver Moon, so they would never be without one another again."

In a triumphant clamor of bells and ringing notes from the *ranad ek*, the torches suddenly blazed up again, even brighter than before. The Sun and his radiant Moon seemed to float across the stage as the entire audience erupted into applause and cheers. The King remained leaning so that his arm rested beside Anna's on the bench.

And suddenly she could feel him there, all around her, as earlier she had sensed his place in the world he ruled. As the bells chimed and people began streaming from the temple grounds, she looked up, unable to keep her gaze from his, and for one long moment they stared, unattended and enraptured, into each other's eyes.

"Your Majesty?"

It was an attendant's voice that broke the spell, ringing out too loudly above the nighttime calm that once more enveloped the *wat*. For an instant the King refused to tear his gaze from Anna's. Then he turned away.

"Yes?"

"Lord Ranya is awaiting you in your tent, Your Majesty."

The King nodded. Without a word to Anna, he stood and left the viewing platform. Anna watched him until his golden festival finery was just another flame-colored spark in the night. Then she stood, her expression unusually subdued, and called to her son.

"Come, Louis. We too must leave now."

And they walked in silence to their tent.

Not everyone was feeling as subdued as Anna that evening. At the edge of the rice fields, scores of palace guards stood around small fires, smoking and talking in low voices, many of them engaged in the endless games of chance that occupied their waking hours. Occasionally someone would cry out, in excitement or displeasure at the way a wager had ended. Then their voices would fade into the twilight susurrus of crickets and frogs, the sharp cries of hunting owls and the far-off shriek of a clouded leopard.

In her own tent, Anna had her hands full. She had already dressed in her long cotton nightgown and pulled her hair into a cap when Louis's groans sounded from behind the curtain that separated them.

"What is it?" she cried, yanking the curtain aside. Louis rolled over, moaning, his face green with nausea; then choked out the dread word.

"Cigar—Prince gave me—cigar—"

"Honestly, Louis! I leave you alone for *five minutes*—"

"It was his idea," Louis protested weakly.

"Just because Prince Chulalongkorn jumps off a bridge doesn't mean you have to."

Louis nodded miserably. "How can anyone *smoke* those things?"

Anna fussed with his mosquito netting, ran a hand along his forehead. "Your father certainly seemed to enjoy them." She paused, smiling at the memory. "Along with a brandy, every now and again."

134

Louis looked at his mother. After a moment he asked, "Is that why you like him? The King, I mean. Because he reminds you of Father?"

Anna's smile disappeared. "Oh, that's rubbish," she said briskly, and turned away.

"He likes you."

"I think that cigar has clouded your brain, young man." She turned down the lamp and gazed at him once more, shaking her head. "In the next five minutes I would like to see you *asleep*."

Prince Chulalongkorn was more fortunate—he was in a clearing in the royal encampment's military compound, where even at this late hour soldiers were loading pistols from barrels of gunpowder, and other young boys amused themselves by hefting cannonballs under the watchful eyes of their elders. The Crown Prince was wrestling with his uncle, Prince Chowfa. On the sidelines the King and General Alak watched, smiling and occasionally commenting when one of the mock combatants executed a particularly graceful move.

"Very good!" the general called to Prince Chulalongkorn. Then, to the King: "He will make as fine a wrestler as his uncle someday."

The King nodded. Overhearing the compliment, Prince Chowfa glanced up, then stiffened. Chulalongkorn slid away from him, the two staring as the Kralahome approached the King, a troubled look on his face.

"Your Majesty—" The Kralahome stopped. He looked around the clearing, then gestured at the armory tent. "I think perhaps we should speak inside . . ."

The King nodded and stood. At the sight of his father's expression, Prince Chulalongkorn bowed and backed away. The others waited as the King entered the tent, and followed him.

"Our nobles are demanding protection," the Kralahome began. "No one knows where these butchers will strike next."

"Then we must strike back, and with twice the venom!" Prince Chowfa said hotly.

"Strike who, my brother?" The King shook his head. "This enemy still has no form."

But Prince Chowfa was not easily silenced. "Loyalists to the King are strung up to rot. Merchants who reject the British are murdered in their beds. England may hide behind Burmese assassins, but the stench is still British!"

The King considered his brother's words, then looked at the counsel-general. "One of us is wrong about the British."

The general was too respectful to disagree. Instead he only nodded, and turned as though to leave. "I will assemble the officers at once."

"No." The King raised a hand. "If you are right about them, this 'war' cannot be won on a battle-field."

Prince Chowfa groaned in frustration. "Your Majesty, if we do not stop these colonial predators, who will?"

The King stared pensively out the door of the tent, to where the crimson embers of a dozen cooking fires could still be seen glowing within the military compound. "If they are as hungry as we fear," he said, crossing his arms, "perhaps it would be wise to first offer them dinner."

The next morning the royal family returned to the palace, and the day after that classes proceeded as usual for the royal children. At her desk inside the Temple of the Mothers of the Free, Anna was giving a physics lesson. Her students watched raptly as she set fire to a piece of lined writing paper, then held it up alongside an empty wine bottle on which a hard-boiled egg was balanced.

"Now, we all know this egg will never fit into this bottle," Anna said sensibly. "It is a fact. It is the truth. And we rely on the truth to make judgments, don't we?"

The children nodded, trying with some difficulty to restrain their excitement.

"But what if our judgment is wrong?" Anna waved the lit paper, leaving a trail of bluish smoke in its wake. "Even when we know, for a fact, that it's right—like this egg. Do we trust our instincts, or . . ."

With a flourish she picked up the egg and waved the flaming paper over the mouth of the bottle. ". . . believe in the impossible!"

The children stared as she replaced the egg. Then, to their amazement, with a resounding *thoooop* the egg was sucked into the bottle.

"You see?" Anna had to raise her voice to be heard among the children's delighted chatter. "All one need do to achieve the impossible is change the climate! The fire consumes the air inside the . . ."

Her voice died as her gaze locked with that of King Mongkut, standing at the back of the classroom with his retinue behind him. She flushed.

The children turned to see what had alarmed her, and with a flurry of chairs and feet they threw themselves onto the floor. The King's gaze swept over them. He said something in Siamese, and as though he had uttered an incantation the children immediately fled the room. Anna looked on helplessly as the King walked over and handed her a newspaper.

"The French say I am 'uncivilized,'" he announced, as though they had begun this conversation ages ago. "I, who have spent entire life attempting to teach self history, literature, and science."

Anna scanned the newspaper. She shook her head. "Why would they print such things?"

"You are English. You should not be so surprised."

He looked down at Anna's pearl-colored dress, her hair carefully drawn into its modest knot at the back of her neck, her feet in their neat calfskin boots. "More important," he said, "do you, as foreigner, see me in this light?"

His gaze did not leave her face. Anna stared back at him, her heart quickening, knowing that no matter how she worded it, her response could be seen as having more than one meaning. "Your Majesty . . . I—I do not know all that you are. But I believe I know what you are *not*, and"—she let the hand holding the newspaper fall to her side—"you are not what they say."

The King gazed at her. "Thank you, Mem, for humble validation," he said softly. Then, "I, um, have decided to give self anniversary dinner, and invite important English nobles and diplomats."

Anna looked confused. "I don't understand."

"French Indochina grows stronger and more aggressive. But if I improve foreign intercourse with your Queen's envoy, French will think three times before trying to undermine Siam."

"Very clever, Your Majesty," said Anna, smiling.

"As if to sound English bugles in own defense." He nodded at her as though something had been decided. "You shall take charge of all formalities, as Mem is obvious choice to make certain guests feel at home."

"And the anniversary is . . . ?"

"Three weeks from yesterday."

"Three weeks!" cried Anna. "But that's impossible!"

The King stared at the desk, where Anna's experiment remained before her. "Mem," he said, pointing at it. "The egg is in the bottle."

seven

A full-scale assault upon the embassies of both France and England would have been easier to organize than the state dinner the King wanted.

Or so Anna thought in the weeks that followed. An army of seamstresses was diverted from their customary work, sewing *panungs* and gowns for the royal wives and concubines, and settled in one of the pavilions adjoining the Temple of the Mothers of the Free. There, with one of Anna's gowns arranged fastidiously upon a makeshift bamboo mannequin, the seamstresses devoted themselves to creating dozens of Western-style ball gowns.

But the subdued hues of Anna's wardrobe did not reign here. The pavilion was a riot of silks and brocades and jacquards, in every shade from jade green to emerald, ivory to scarlet, the rich indigo of a peacock's breast to the aquamarine of the royal lake at dawn. Visitors came and went constantly, concubines and the *Chao Chom Manda,* anxious to try on their new finery. They modeled their gowns for each other, tittering as they struggled with crinolines and the excessive layers of Victorian underthings. Delighted as they were with the gowns, however, many of the women were fearful at the thought of meeting so many *farangs* at once. And so there was a brisk trade in talismans to keep them safe against any *farang* sorcery, as well as the usual complement of amulets against the *phi,* the demons who could torment the wary and unprotected. Nothing Anna could say or do would dissuade the women from arming themselves thus. So it was that when the great evening finally arrived, King Mongkut's consorts were well armored with both silken petticoats and amulets.

King Mongkut's retainers had been busy as well, mastering the intricacies of Western silverware and the baroque turns of English etiquette—whom to address as "Sir" and "Lady," who took precedence at the dining table, who was expressly *not* to be seated next to the French bishop, and why.

Anna took charge of the musical entertainment, teaching her students the words to "Scarborough Fair" and rehearsing them morning and afternoon until they knew every verse by heart. The piano was old and out of tune—tropical heat and moisture played havoc with the keys, and there was not a piano tuner for a thousand miles. But Anna soldiered on, until she imagined she could hear the children's chorus singing to her as she slept, their sweet, high voices echoing through the little brick house until she woke, sweat-drenched, to find herself facing yet another day of preparations.

The anniversary day finally dawned—overcast and hazy, the sky the color of turgid water and smelling of it, too, the overheated vapors from the city's *klongs* hanging in the air in a fine greenish mist. But within an hour the haze had cleared; the sun shone brightly in a laquered-blue sky, yellow-robed monks chanted as holy men read augers in the trail of dust left by the *ngu thong daeng*, the sacred crimson-bellied snake. Anna watched, fascinated, surrounded by the other ladies of the court as they stood within the Temple of the Emerald Buddha, the King's private temple. There was a flurry at the back of the *wat*. Anna looked up, thinking that some of her charges had crept away from Lady Thiang's watchful eye.

Yet it was not a child but Tuptim, come to make her own offering. She prostrated herself before the altar, and several minutes later stood to depart. As she did, the monks lifted their fans to cover their eyes, shielding themselves from her beauty.

The day passed like a dream, as Anna knew it would. There were frantic last-minute arrangements to be made, deliveries of flowers and panniers of fresh fruit, overexcited children to be calmed, women to be dressed.

There were a poignant few minutes while Anna was instructing a room full of servants on how to pour champagne. Without warning, they all dropped to the floor, sending silver trays crashing and bottles flying in their wake, as Anna turned to see the King in the back of the hall. She threw her hands up in frustration, but he took no notice.

"Stand," he commanded loudly. "All of you—*stand!*"

Slowly, with heartbreaking timidity, everyone stood. Anna watched, trying to keep her own emotions in check.

"It is only for a night," the King reminded her as

he gazed disapprovingly upon this room full of upright citizens. "One night—"

And with a scowl, he left.

As dusk settled upon the palace, Anna found herself on the grand outer terrace, arranging a bouquet of orchids, jasmine, and violets in a huge Chinese vase. The weeks of preparation had taken their toll: she was pale with exhaustion, her hair unfurling from where she had pinned it loosely above her neck.

"Mother . . ."

Anna turned, blinking, and saw Louis standing at her elbow. He wore his very best suit and tie, his hair slicked back and his cheeks rosy from scrubbing. It took her a moment to recognize him, and she laughed.

"Goodness! I'm so tired, I thought you were another of the servants!"

"Mother, you have to come, now. The guests are already starting to arrive."

Anna looked over and saw Beebe and Moonshee standing anxiously at the top of the steps. As gingerly as though it were an infant, Beebe held in her arms Anna's gown, a white ball gown frothing with lace and tiny embroidered rosebuds. Anna sighed, drew her hand across her brow, then smiled at her son and took his hand.

"Yes, of course—thank you, Louis . . ." Reluctantly she left her flowers, a slender stalk of yellow orchids trailing down the wall behind her like a tear.

Three hundred and seventy-three servants had been at work since five o'clock that morning, transforming the great Audience Hall into a ballroom suitable for any sixteen heads of state. A mixed bag of British aristocrats and Siamese nobles stood stiffly around the room, sipping champagne from crystal flutes. The royal wives moved among them like so many gorgeously costumed automatons, lifting their feet with exquisite care, wary lest they trip in their unfamiliar new Western shoes. Their hair had been coiffed in the latest Parisian styles—the kindly French bishop had provided copies of newspapers and magazines as models—and some of them wore elaborate blonde and auburn wigs over their own close-cropped tresses. The gowns revealed a daring amount of décolletage; to offset this, many of the women had tucked talismans between their breasts, or sprigs of wild ginger. In one corner, female court musicians played a melancholy air upon their *pins*, and two very young servants released a horde of transparent-winged dragon-tail butterflies from bamboo cages, to flutter above the guests.

Yet despite the banks of orchids, the silk tapestries, and flickering candlelight, an air of eerie quiet filled the splendid hall. King Mongkut's interpreter strolled uneasily through the crowd, attempting small talk with the guests.

But the European guests were too cautious to begin speaking with an unknown Siamese man. Mired between British reserve and the Siamese mistrust of foreigners, the interpreter shrugged, cleared his throat, and began to declaim to the room at large.

"Please forgive nervousness," he announced, looking pointedly at the British attaché. "This is first time in Siam history a king allow everyone to stand in his presence. But only for tonight."

The British attaché smiled politely but said nothing. The interpreter turned to the Siamese nobleman standing beside him. "Did you know that in Britain they once wore uniforms of metal called knights?"

The nobleman's smile was equally polite. The interpreter gritted his teeth, snatched a glass of champagne from a passing tray, and began resolutely to lecture another group.

147

In the center of the room, King Mongkut stood resplendent in his uniform of state. Surrounding him was a small knot of British diplomats, including the distinguished Lord Bradley, a rugged, white-haired man in his sixties, and his gentle-spoken wife, Lady Bradley. The Kralahome had joined them a few minutes earlier, his wary expression ill-suited to their magnificent surroundings, as well as General Alak and the defiant Prince Chowfa, who stared balefully at his brother.

"Your country and mine have much in common, Your Majesty," said Lord Bradley. He raised his champagne glass and smiled at his host. "Rich culture, long histories, and now, it seems, Madam Leonowens."

The King nodded. "Yes, my children's horizons keep expanding under her tutelage."

"My husband and I have been stationed all over the world," said Lady Bradley with a disarming smile. "But I must say, I've never seen anything quite like this."

She gestured at the room around them, butterflies like colored smoke wafting overhead.

General Alak nodded. "Grand Palace born from the mind of King Taksin, first man to unify all of

Siam. Our country owes its creation to a man they called insane."

"Well, these rooftops *are* a little nutty," said Lady Bradley.

"He endeavored to build an empire," the general continued, "but nobility that ran Siam for generations had grown tired of war and betrayed him. He was put in a velvet sack, beaten to death, and buried somewhere in the palace."

Stunned by his blunt words, Lady Bradley took a moment to come up with a reply. "It sounds to me, General, as though you admired him."

"I admire vision," the general said obliquely, and glanced away. "Ah, but see this . . ."

As though a wind stirred the room, a hush passed over the assembled guests. The King turned with the others, his face alight as he spied Anna's slim figure making its way discreetly through the side entrance. She edged through the crowd, finally stopping before their group. She tilted her head at the King, then curtsied, her dress forming a dazzling white pool around her as she sank to the floor.

"Forgive me, Your Majesty, but I believe the sun set a little earlier today."

Anna stood, her face aglow in the light of twenty

thousand wax candles. She looked ravishing, all the fatigue of the previous weeks swept aside in the glory of the King's success—and her own. The King could not tear his gaze from her. After a moment he realized he was not alone in this, and a twinge of jealousy passed across his strong face. He struggled to maintain calm as he spoke.

"Mem, you arrange all this"—he extended his hand to indicate the well-dressed throng, the tables piled with orchids and the delicate butteflies soaring above them—"all this to influence positive future of Siam, and now you steal attention away from it."

Anna blushed. "That was not my intention, Your Majesty."

"Madam Leonowens!" cried Lord Bradley, oblivious of the Kralahome and Prince Chowfa scowling behind him. "What a delightful surprise, encountering such an enchanting countryman so far from home."

Anna bowed as Lord Bradley took her hand. "Lord Bradley. This is indeed a great honor."

"And you, my dear," said Lady Bradley, "however do you manage?"

Anna smiled at her host. "His Majesty has been most gracious."

From outside came a sudden fanfare, *pi* and bamboo *khaen* summoning the revelers to dinner. The entire gathering turned and began making its way up the red-carpeted concourse to where dozens of servnts in white linen stood waiting on the carpeted steps. Anna escorted Lady Bradley, who was craning her head like a tourist at St. Paul's.

Anna nodded. "Extraordinary, isn't it?"

Lady Bradley could only nod vigorously in reply.

The King's anniversary dinner consisted of twenty-seven courses, all served by a host of servants in white and crimson livery. Louis and the royal children serenaded the diners with "Scarborough Fair," accompanied not by Anna's rusty piano but by the plangent notes of the court musicians plucking their *khaen* and the richer tone of the *ranad ek*. King Mongkut sat at the head of the long U-shaped table, flanked by Lord Bradley and his wife to the right, the Kralahome, Anna, and Prince Chowfa to his left. Overhead the starry sky unfolded, a glittering carpet of blue and violet and silver; beneath it, the city glowed by the light of ten thousand lanterns. As Anna listened to the children, her eyes welled with tears. When they finished singing, she joined the other guests in tumultuous applause.

"Gracious ladies and kind sirs . . ."

Prince Chulalongkorn stepped forward from the assembled children, bowing to the guests. "On behalf of sixty-eight brothers and sisters, we thank you immeasurably and bid you most gracious evening."

The King beamed with pride as the other royal children (and Louis) exited to more applause and the guests turned their attention back to their feast.

"Your young man bears a striking resemblance to his father, Mrs. Leonowens."

Anna carefully placed her fork down and turned. A handsome young Englishman in military dress uniform sat at a nearby table, smiling. Beside him was the ethereally beautiful, and somber, Lady Tuptim.

"Captain Blake, is it?" asked Anna.

He nodded. "You have a fine memory. I had the good fortune of serving with your husband a few years back. He was a courageous soldier, ma'am."

Anna's eyes filled. "Thank you, Captain Blake."

He tipped his head and turned away. Anna sat for a moment, silent, unaware of the King's gaze upon her.

"Father!"

Heads turned. Alone on the terrace, where the

children had sung, the little Princess Fa-Ying stood. "Father? May I please kiss good night?"

A chorus of delighted *Aaaahs* from the crowd. The King smiled and stood, addressing his guests. "If I may beg indulgence for not wishing to break family tradition . . ." He beckoned to the Princess.

Without a sound she raced across the terrace, leapt into his arms, and hugged him. "I will be there in your dreams, *looja*," the King whispered, lifting a strand of hair from her ear, "as you will be in mine."

The little girl kissed him again, then jumped from his arms and ran back inside.

"You have a remarkable family," an Englishman announced loudly. Anna recognized the business-man Mycroft Kincaid, swaying slightly as he motioned at a servant to refill his glass. "A remark-ably *large* one. Why, it hardly seems fair, all these women for one man." He chortled drunkenly. "Makes me wish I were Siamese myself."

Anna and the Bradleys glanced away, embar-rassed, but King Mongkut gave him a keen look.

"Mycroft Kincaid of East India Company, correct?"

Kincaid took a swig from his glass. He nodded, blotting his lips with a linen napkin. "Guilty as charged, Your Majesty."

Lord Bradley broke in smoothly. "Mr. Kincaid's company is one of the ways we try to foster economic relations with other countries, Your Majesty."

King Mongkut regarded the Englishmen icily. "Also, I think, to arrive at forefront of world in wealth and power, yes?"

All eyes focused on the subtle duel taking place at the King's table. Anna tensed. She played with the napkin in her lap, waiting to see how the Englishman responded. Even the Kralahome looked disconcerted as King Mongkut turned to Lord Bradley.

But the King only reached across the table, picking up several salt cellars shaped like Siamese gondolas, and began aranging them in front of him. "Lord Bradley, what would you say is most prominent building material in boat-building process?"

"Why, wood, of course."

"And most valuable for such is teak—tree native to Siam but rare in rest of world."

Captain Blake looked at Lord Bradley and nodded. "Teak ships sail for generations."

King Mongkut continued. "Gentleman, Siam is country rich with resources already traded with Eastern neighbors but not with the West. With ever shifting political stage, and increasing French influence, expanding existing trade agreements with you on teak and other commodities could strengthen the bridge between our two countries. England saves money. Makes money. Gains consulate. And grows even stronger. Siam's economy is cultivated to benefit its people, built on trust as tall and strong as newly planted forests where isolated trees once stood."

Inspired, Lord Bradley leaned forward, chin in hand, as Anna offered the King an encouraging smile.

"With all due respect, Your Majesty," Kincaid broke in, his voice thick with drink, "it is a little far-fetched to believe commerce alone will bring progress to your people."

All heads turned to the indelicate businessman. "Especially when they're awash in superstition and fear, like your lovely princesses here with their talismans." Kincaid leered at Tuptim, then took a sip of wine. "Worn, no doubt, to protect them from us foreign devils."

The King smiled disarmingly. "A friend once said, Mr. Kincaid, that English also have fantastical beliefs . . ." He nodded at his English guests. "Or am I mistaking your country for being land of Merlin and Camelot?"

Anna dipped her head, hoping that no one would notice her blush, or realize that she was indeed that "friend." Around her, the Bradleys and other English diplomats gave each other furtive looks, hoping that Mycroft Kincaid would have the good sense to back off.

He did not. "Point taken, Your Majesty." He raised his glass in an unsteady toast. "However, there is no arguing the superiority of the English. And in light of those dreadful massacres up and down your border, it's no wonder you're seeking our favor."

Anger flared in King Mongkut's eyes. He started to rise. The Kralahome watched expectantly, and Prince Chowfa laid a hand on his sword. Suddenly Anna's voice rang out through the hall.

"Superiority, Mr. Kincaid?" All eyes snapped to her. "I don't recall anyone being given the right to judge whose culture or customs are superior—especially when those judging have frequently imposed themselves at the point of a gun. Wouldn't you agree, Your Majesty?"

The Kralahome gazed dumbfounded at this foreign woman's defense of their country. So did General Alak and Prince Chowfa. King Mongkut turned to Anna as well, his anger deflected by her passionate words.

Lord Bradley tugged at his collar and said diplomatically, "Well, the evenings here certainly are a bit *warmer* than in London . . ."

There was a chiming chorus of "Here, here!" from the English guests. Anna, realizing she might have overstepped her bounds, turned from the drunken Kincaid to find the King scrutinizing her.

"I agree," Prince Chowfa announced, nodding at Lord Bradley. "A night made to order for anniversary party."

King Mongkut turned back to his guests. *"Especially* for a king who is most tolerant and forgiving."

The English guests smiled with relief. The Siamese contingent exchanged quietly triumphant looks, settling back and murmuring as they began to eat once more. In her seat, Anna stared down at her plate, feeling her face burn and fighting the almost irresistible urge to gaze at King Mongkut.

And even without looking, she could sense, somehow, that he was doing the same. She swallowed, her mouth dry; picked up her fork, dropped it; struggled to contain herself. In the last few minutes she had crossed a threshold—of what, even Anna herself was not sure. But she feared to know, feared to look too deeply inside her heart, lest she see eyes that were not her husband's gazing out at her—eyes that would hold her own if only she lifted her head and gazed across the table.

A good-natured voice broke her reverie. "Have only met you tonight, Mem, but feel comfortable requesting to sharpen English with you."

It was Prince Chowfa, grinning broadly as he raised his glass to her. "So I, too, might add language to my arsenal."

Anna smiled. Across from them, Lord Bradley stood, lifting his glass and calling out in a clear voice, "To our host—a true gentleman, generous in every way!"

Everyone rose, hoisting their glasses as Lord Bradley went on. "May history mark this occasion as the first step toward forging an alliance between our two countries."

"Here, here!"

The guests drank. King Mongkut observed them,

smiling, then got to his feet and motioned at the court musicians. The hollow notes of the *ranak ek* died away. A moment as the musicians paused, adjusting their instruments. Then, to Anna's astonishment, the plaintive strains of a waltz filled the Great Hall.

King Mongkut's smile broadened at her surprise.

"In honor of our most distinguished guests, a waltz, as is European custom of dancing after dinner."

Caught off guard, Anna stared at the King. Slowly he extended his hand to her, holding her gaze as she hesitated and then, nodding slightly, put her hand into his. As the entire assembly—British and Siamese alike—watched in amazement, the Lord of Life escorted the British schoolteacher to the center of the terrace.

"I—I think you should know, Your Majesty," stammered Anna as the King led her. "But I haven't . . . *waltzed* in some time. And, well, with things going as well as they are, we wouldn't want to end up in a heap, would we?"

The King stared at her. His smile was warm, but in his eyes a greater heat glowed as he drew her to him.

"I am King. *I* shall lead."

He placed his other hand upon her waist and, more gracefully than she could have imagined, began to lead her through the waltz. Guests watched mesmerized as they whirled past, Anna's white gown fairly incandescent in the torchlight, and as they moved through the room, other guests joined them. First Lord Bradley and his wife, and then another couple, and another, until the terrace glimmered and shone with hundreds of swirling shapes, magical as the dragon-tail butterflies soaring overhead. Only the Kralahome and General Alak watched stonily, while beside them Prince Chowfa stared at his brother and the schoolteacher, enchanted.

"I have never danced with an Englishwoman before, Mem," King Mongkut murmured as they swept past the musicians.

Anna's rapturous smile was met by his own. "I am honored, Your Majesty."

"I want you to make promise, Mem—to always tell King what you think. No matter what. Like to man from East India Company."

An instant as they swooped and turned, and then Anna replied, "I always have."

And the King and the schoolteacher gazed at one

another blissfully, as though they were the only waltzing couple upon the terrace—and to the watchful, joyous eyes of Princess Fa-Ying, watching them from her hidden perch upon the terrace, they were.

eight

"Memsahib?"

Anna nodded absently at Beebe's voice and adjusted the bundle she held cradled in her arms. Around them stretched the noisy, bright glory of Pratunam Market, with its fruit stalls and fishermen displaying that morning's catch, fish still gasping and twitching in bamboo baskets, flower vendors with their wreaths of orchids and more humble blossoms, weavers unfurling bolts of printed silk and cotton. The air was thick with the scents of cooking—pungent *nam pha*, the fermented fish sauce the Siamese poured on everything; the warm, steamy smell of sticky rice; the head-clearing odor of *prik*, chilis in profusion, an entire rainbow of them: little yellow chilis, orange and red and purple ones, peppers in every shade of green and the miniscule *prik-kee-nu*, "mouse-droppings." Anna paused, gazing absently at a flat basket full of violet-colored fermented shrimp balls, then looked up with a start into Beebe's penetrating gaze.

"Memsahib?" Beebe said again, a little louder.

"Yes?"

"You're . . . *humming.*"

Anna straightened, letting a tiny naked toddler pass, and shifted her parcels. "I suppose I am." She smiled. "As alarming as this may sound, Beebe, I'm feeling rather at home here. Such gentle people. Remember when this market used to terrify us?"

Beebe nodded. "Like it was yesterday." She wiped her brow, smoothing her damp hair. "I was afraid that dinner might have unsettled you. All those Englishmen in uniform."

"Yes. I thought it would make me miserably homesick, but it was quite the opposite. I think I enjoyed myself. Even the dancing."

She picked up a small woven basket, seawater dripping from it, and peered at the blue and pink shrimp nestled inside on a bed of kelp. "I think we should try some of these, don't you?"

Beebe agreed, and they went on to the next booth.

"And how did His Majesty fare amongst all your countrymen?"

Anna laughed. "Quite charming, actually. I will never forget the way he stood here holding his hand out to me. Like I was . . ."

"One of his twenty-six wives?"

Anna gave Beebe an odd look, then laughed again. "Thank you, Beebe. I hadn't thought about it in quite that way."

Beebe gazed at her sharply. When she spoke, her tone was warning. "Well, perhaps you should."

Anna said nothing. After a moment she nodded and turned. She was heading for a vendor selling baskets when suddenly a hand plucked at her sleeve. She looked down to see a young boy, his bare legs covered with dust, smiling up at her as he held out a bamboo tube.

"Yes?"

The boy smiled, mimed something that Anna could not comprehend, then with a laugh whirled and raced off. Puzzled, she watched him go, and finally examined the tube. It was a sort of envelope, inside which a small parchment scroll could be rolled. Someone had written a name on the outside, in very small, fine black English letters.

KHUN JAO TUPTIM

Anna frowned. A letter for Tuptim? From the family she had spoken of so fervently? She looked around, vainly trying to recognize the sender somewhere in the crowd. At last she gave up and, sighing, followed Beebe through the marketplace.

Back within the Hidden City, four royal concubines sat sharing a half dozen durians as they traded tales and gossiped. The durians were a globular fruit covered with spikes, like immense green horse chestnuts, but when a servant peeled them, their sweet, custardy inner flesh was revealed, ivory-colored and sweet as stewed mangos. The durians' odor, however, was anything but sweet—a ripe, ammoniac scent like raw sewage—and the concubines squealed, ordering the servant from their room to scoop the delicacy into small bowls to be savored later.

"Idiot! Preparing durian inside—one would think he had never peeled one before!"

The other concubines nodded, rolling their eyes. One peered from the room to check on the durians' progress, then returned to the other women.

"His Majesty has not visited me in two months." She settled back beside the others and picked a betel nut from a brass tray. "Two months!"

"He's too busy 'studying' the English," an older woman said slyly.

"What do you think they talk about?"

The older concubine shrugged. "He's a man, she's a woman. Who said anything about talk?"

The first woman shook her head, puzzled. "But she's *English*."

Abruptly they all dissolved in laughter. At that moment the oldest concubine sighted Anna approaching down the corridor. She leaned forward, hushing her friends. They all smiled sweetly as Anna crossed and entered Tuptim's room.

The young concubine was standing at her window, gazing out upon one of the Women's Gardens, where tiny green sparrows darted and a lone peahen paced slowly back and forth, back and forth.

"Tuptim?"

She started from her reverie, then turned, palms pressed together as she gazed respectfully at Anna.

"I have a surprise for you."

She handed the bamboo tube to her. As Tuptim read the name inscribed there, her eyes widened. "How did you . . . ?"

Anna smiled. "Actually, I'm not quite sure."

Tuptim *wai*ed deeply. "Thank you, Mem. My . . . family is very important to me."

"Then I shall leave you to enjoy every word."

As she left, Tuptimn stared down at the message from her lover, her eyes welling.

The rest of the week passed so slowly that once again Anna imagined she was back on board the *Newcastle*, dreaming of a home port. She castigated herself for her naïveté, yet still she had hoped there might be *some* word from the King. The children were inordinately cheerful—the rehearsals for the anniversary dinner had brought them all closer for a few weeks, and its enchantment remained even now that the great event had passed.

But when Friday came, there was—at last!—a message for Anna to see the King that evening. She dressed with particular care that morning: she would not go so far as to change clothes before their meeting, but not even Beebe could argue that it was important to look her best for a royal audience. The day fairly crept by, but finally she dismissed her students, ate a rushed meal, and as dusk fell, hurried down the corridor toward the King's study.

It was the first time she had been permitted in this

part of the palace. She smoothed her hair nervously as the door opened.

"Mem?"

Nikorn, the King's bodyguard, stood beckoning her to enter. Anna nodded and walked inside.

Heavens! She drew her breath in, flabbergasted at the display around her. Telescopes, microscopes, instruments she could not name, or even imagine what purpose they might serve—a veritable treasure house of marvels, all devoted to science. The walls were covered with bookshelves and laden with volumes, many in European languages; but there were also some parchment scrolls and cotton tapestries of obvious and great antiquity. A cigar lay in a vast marble ashtray, sending a thin trail of blue smoke to the ceiling high above; but of the King there was no sign.

"Your Majesty?" A pair of great double doors opened out onto the balcony. Gingerly Anna stepped through them, blinking as she tried to make out a figure in the twilight. "Your—"

And there he was, standing at the balustrade and gazing at the scene below. At the sound of her voice he turned, slowly. Their eyes met, and for a moment there was silence. Then Anna looked away awkwardly and cleared her throat.

"You sent for me?"

"Yes, but here—look."

She joined him at the balustrade, the two of them peering through a leafy canopy of rhododendrons into the Children's Garden. A tiny figure in a white dress twirled and dipped along the path, stopping at the edge of the reflecting pool and curtsying, then continuing her solitary, soundless waltz.

"Fa-Ying . . ." whispered Anna, her heart melting.

"Something tells me my little waltzing monkey did not go to bed night of anniversary."

Anna nodded. "Yes, I know. I have been presented with drawings of couples dancing ever since."

For a minute they stood side by side, staring into the purple twilight, the night air soft with the smell of jasmine and the twittering of sparrows nesting for the night. Then, abruptly, the King turned and headed back inside. He withdrew his spectacles and put them on, marched behind his desk, and began shuffling through papers. Startled, Anna waited, then followed him. He glanced at her perfunctorily and gestured at some pillows.

"Sit, please." With some effort he summoned a smile. "I do not think it shall be damaging to most handsome attire."

Anna smiled back tentatively, rearranged her skirts, and sat. The King continued sorting through his desk, and she watched, wondering what had happened to bring on this mood. When he still ignored her, she shrugged and tried to make conversation.

"I—our home, Your Majesty . . . the garden is in full bloom and, well, I would be deeply honored if one day you might join us for afternoon tea."

The King smoothed out a sheaf of documents. With a nod he looked down at her. "This is British custom, yes?"

Anna smiled. "Yes. It's one of our little English eccentricities. You can learn a lot about someone over tea."

He regarded her for such a long time that she began to fear she had said the wrong thing. Finally he said, "Perhaps if our calendars allow, as I know you also have been busy."

"Every day seems to bring no shortage of new challenges."

"And questions of much difficulty with far too few answers."

Anna looked puzzled, trying to tease the meaning from this. The two of them stared at each other. For a moment the King looked as though he were about to continue. Instead he turned his attention back to his papers. Anna studied him, unsure as to whether she should interfere, then hesitantly spoke.

"Your Majesty, it might be easier to talk about what you're trying so hard *not* to."

The King stared at her. Then, sighing, he removed his glasses and rubbed his eyes.

"I share this with you, Mem, because I believe you to be trustworthy." He spoke slowly, as though each word cost him more effort than the last. "Events are happening which I now believe to be of Burmese origin, and I fear that military action is unavoidable."

"But—Burma is British?"

"Yes."

Anna drew a hand to her forehead as the truth slowly began to dawn. "Then, it wasn't the French you were worried about, was it?"

The King shook his head. "I had hoped your country would extend hand of friendship, given relation we try to forge, but all we hear is silence."

"I see."

He had used her. The anniversary party, her weeks of preparations, the waltz—it had all been part of a plan of which she had known nothing, nothing at all. Anna felt as though she had been slapped. Not knowing what else to say, she rose and slowly headed for the door.

But before she reached it, the King spoke again. He did not look up.

"On table, Mem, is small gift of appreciation for your many efforts at anniversary party."

Anna stopped, then turned and walked over to the table. There, on a small silver tray, was a magnificent golden ring, clustered with emeralds, its face etched with the symbols of the Sun and the Moon.

Anna had to keep herself from gasping. Behind her, the King's hand moved across a page. There was the muted scraching of a quill pen. Her reserve melting, Anna slowly reached for the ring, but as her fingers hovered above it she hesitated.

"You—you are most kind, Your Majesty," she said. Her voice broke and she blinked, looking away. "And it is very, very beautiful . . . and while I am terribly grateful . . ."

From the table, the scratching of the quill pen continued uninterrupted. "It is custom to bestow favors on those who please King," he said, still preoccupied. "And Mem has done so."

"I—I'm sorry. I . . . cannot accept such . . . such generosity."

The pen fell silent. King Mongkut looked up. His eyes met Anna's and held them, for a long, long time, while outside the twilight deepened and the first bats began stitching across the sky. At last Anna curtsied silently and left. It was longer still before the King picked up his pen again. When he did, his hand trembled, ever so slightly, as it moved across the page.

nine

She buried her heartache with work. What else could she do? The children needed her; it was why she had come to Bangkok, after all — to teach the children of a king, not to let her head be turned by torchlight and jasmine and the strains of a waltz. As the days passed, the weather shifted, as though accommodating her mood: it grew warm and sultry, and she exchanged her heavy taffetas for the lighter cotton dresses she had worn in Bombay during the summer.

In the heat, the Temple of the Mothers of the Free grew so stuffy that the children drooped. The smaller ones fell asleep at their desks; the older boys became querulous and prone to fistfights. So she moved the entire class outdoors, setting up a temporary laboratory at the edge of the royal lake, where the children caught tadpoles and examined water lilies under one of their father's magnifying lenses. When they tired of this, Anna got some of the bigger boys to help her prepare a makeshift cricket field on one of the palace lawns. The girls painted a banner—SIAMESE CRICKET CLUB—and she took the opportunity to turn the game into an impromptu physics lesson, shouting above the children's excited cheers.

"And Newton's third law of motion states that for every action . . ."

Prince Chulalongkorn stood at the wicket, holding Louis's bat, as Anna took her place on the bowling crease. She smiled, shading her eyes from the afternoon sun, and cried, ". . . there is an equal and opposite reaction."

She performed her windup, grinning at the Crown Prince's intent expression, then bowled the ball.

Thwack!

The ball went rocketing over the trees, the children screaming with delight as they raced after it.

"Jolly good, Your Highness!" yelled Louis. "Now—run!"

Anna wiped her brow and sought shelter in the scant shade of a palm tree. When she glanced up, she saw a small group of figures on the portico of the Grand Palace: King Mongkut and his ministers. It was too far away for her to see him clearly, but his face was turned toward hers. Before she could lift her hand in greeting, though, he turned and receded into the Audience Hall.

"The heat will not last," Lady Thiang had told Anna after the fifth straight day of temperatures over a hundred degrees. Anna had thought her words were meant to be comforting. As it turned out, they were more of a warning. When the heat broke, it broke with a vengeance, and in its stead the monsoons began. Classes were conducted in a small side wing of the *Khang nai*, where every morning Anna and Louis arrived bedraggled after their brief journey from home. Their clothes would barely have time to dry before they returned each afternoon. Finally, the rains grew so severe that class was cancelled. The royal children were left to the care of their mothers and nurses, and Louis and Anna sought shelter in the little brick house.

Tuptim, however, did not let the rains stop her

from venturing out. Alone, and furtively, she slipped through narrow streets where water rushed as through a *klong*, until she reached the Temple of the Emerald Buddha. There she stood near the main gate, heedless of the rain soaking her clothes as she waited . . .

And finally saw what she had sought: a long procession of monks in saffron robes, their faces obscured by the bamboo umbrellas they carried against the relentless monsoon. Tuptim craned her neck desperately, trying to see past the umbrellas.

He was not there. He was not there.

Then the very last monk stepped through the gate, paused, and looked back at her. The doors began to close, but in that fleeting instant she recognized him—despite the shaven head and eyebrows, despite the anguished look he gave her. She had never seen such sorrow and desolation in a face before. To meet it in the eyes of her beloved was too much for her to bear. As the gates of the monastery shut upon Balat, Tuptim buried her face in her hands and gave herself utterly to her grief.

Yet even as the days passed and still the monsoon swept across the palace grounds, the ache in Anna's breast subsided. She was not a child like Tuptim. She would not waste her life mooning over some imaginary dalliance; she was a grown woman, with a child and an entire romantic life behind her. And the King was a man much older than herself, with ministers and generals to occupy his days, and scores of wives his nights. She had not seen him in almost two weeks now. If sometimes late at night the image of the King's face came to her, gazing from across a candlelit table, she knew the image to be a fancy, nothing more, bred of boredom and the endless tapping of rain at the eaves.

She sat one evening on the veranda, the warmth of the monsoon sending trailers of mist across the garden. Inside, Beebe and Moonshee clattered about making dinner, and Louis stomped around the living room, tootling loudly on his little brass bugle.

"I hardly think ten days of rain warrants the call to battle, Louis," Anna chided.

Moonshee poked his head out from the kitchen. "May I suggest retreat?"

"Mother," said Louis firmly, "I think I should have a topknot like Prince Chulalongkorn."

Anna rolled her eyes. "I think you have gone a bit daft, darling."

Beebe nodded. "With all this rain, it's no wonder."

"I don't see why I have to miss school," Louis fumed.

"Because your classroom is under water," said Anna. "Come, let's get ready for dinner."

Late that night, she woke from a dream of storm-tossed oceans and a lone bird crying overhead. She sat up, hearing only the insistent rattle of a loose shutter striking the side of the house. She clambered out from beneath the mosquito netting and crossed to the window, securing the latch, and on the way back to bed noticed something fluttering across the floor. A large moth, she thought at first, but as she drew near it, she saw that it was one of Fa-Ying's bright drawings, torn loose from where she had tacked it to the wall. Anna picked it up, smiling, felt another, deeper pang. It had been ten days since she'd seen the little Princess—too long. She sighed, looked around to see a number of the child's drawings drifting across the floor, like so many blown petals. She picked them up, one by one, then brought them to her bedside table. There she laid them carefully beside the tintype of her husband and went back to sleep.

• • •

Sleep did not come to the King that night, and had not for many, many days now. As rain tore at the roofs of the palace, he sought solace and divine intervention within that holiest of places, the Temple of the Emerald Buddha. It was traditionally the King's private haven, and tonight once more found him there alone, bathed in a halo of candlelight, a pale cloud of incense rising from burners set at the four cardinal points. On the altar, a small carven figure of solid jade sat upon a pyramid of gold. Heaps of flowers lay before it, some of them tattered and wilted, others only recently laid there as offerings. The King knelt before the Buddha in silence, bowing reverently once and then again as he whispered prayers and invocations.

But on the third bow, he did not rise. His body sagged as, relentlessly as the rain, sobs wracked his body, and the King wept as though his heart would break.

The next morning, the monsoons stopped. As a pale sun climbed in the watery sky, Louis and Moonshee busied themselves outside, repairing a little spirit house that had been damaged by the storm. On the veranda, Anna and Beebe hung out sheets to dry.

"It will take weeks for everything to air out again," Anna sighed.

"Memsahib?" Anna looked down as Moonshee called to her questioning. "We have visitors."

From the path leading to the river a small procession appeared: a royal messenger and a quartet of palace guards in full dress uniform. The messenger's face was anxious, almost frightened, and Anna stared, disquieted, before hurrying outside to meet them.

Neither Louis nor Moonshee nor Beebe could hear their conversation, but minutes later Anna was rushing back into the house, grabbing a shawl before running outside again.

"Mother! What is it?"

Anna stopped as Louis ran up to her, his face white. "I must go," she said, hugging him to her.

"But what—"

"I want you to pray, Louis." Her arms tightened around him. "As hard as you can."

He nodded. She kissed his forehead, then followed the messenger to the river. It was only after they were out of sight that Louis noticed the white scrap of paper fluttering in front of the spirit house. Tentatively he picked it up and began to read.

My dear Mam,

Our well-beloved daughter, your favourite pupil, is attacked with cholera, and has earnest desire to see you, and is heard much to make frequent repetition of your name. I beg that you will favour her wish. I fear her illness is mortal, as there has been three deaths since morning. She is best beloved of my children.

I am your afflicted friend,
S.S.P.P Maha Mongkut

The Kralahome met her at the entrance to the King's private chambers. The hallway was dimly lit, and rows of guards waited at attention as she walked quickly after the Prime Minister. At the end of the corridor a door stood open, and from inside the faint sound of chanting echoed eerily.

"Cholera always in world, but still hardly at all in Bangkok," the Kralahome was saying, his voice tight.

"Is there nothing you can do?" asked Anna desperately.

He shook his head. "They have already begun. Listen." From inside, the chanting grew louder and more urgent. "'*Phra Arahan*'—reminding soul to go to heaven and not lose way."

They reached the door. Anna covered her face with her hands and began to shake. The Kralahome touched her, very gently, on the arm.

"It is why Mem must not be heard weeping, as soul will attach to sadness and remain to comfort living." Anna nodded, eyes shut, as the Kralahome added, "His Majesty will be grateful. Little one has been making frequent mention of sir's name."

They entered the King's chamber. The room was dark and shrouded with incense. Along the back wall, a small gathering of relatives and servants knelt, chanting. Lady Thiang was among them, too overcome to do more than whisper the sacred syllables over and over again.

"Phra arahan . . . phra arahan . . ."

In the center of the room, on a low platform, sat King Mongkut. Cradled in his arms was the Princess Fa-Ying. Her eyes were closed tight, her features pale, almost translucent, a sheen of sweat giving her skin an eerie glow. A wizened monk knelt beside her, passing his thin fingers back and forth over her brow, his lips moving in prayer.

In the doorway stood Anna, her heart breaking. She drew a long breath, then walked slowly across the room to where the King sat.

"Fa-Ying," she whispered.

She knelt beside the King, gazing down at the tiny Princess's face. For a moment even the chanting seemed to grow silent, and then Fa-Ying's eyes opened. She stared at Anna, and then recognition flickered in her gaze. Like a shadow, the faintest of smiles stirred her face. Then she turned back to her father, nestling against his breast with a sigh. King Mongkut bent to kiss her forehead, shutting his eyes as the tears began to fall. When he opened them again, the Princess Fa-Ying was still.

"*Pai sawan na*," he whispered. "*Chao-fa-ying-cha*." *Make your way heavenward, Fa-Ying.*

To all the foreign friends of His Majesty residing or trading in Siam, or in Singapore, Malacca, Penang, Ceylon, Batavia, Saigon, Macao, Hong Kong, & various regions in China, Europe, America, &c., &c. . . .

The Moreover very sad & mournful Circular from His Gracious Majesty Somdetch P'hra Paramendr Maha Mongkut, the reigning Supreme King of Siam, intimating the recent death of Her Celestial Royal Highness, Princess Somdetch Chowfa Chandrmondol Sobhon Baghiawati. . . .

The sudden death of the said most affectionate and lamented Royal daughter has caused greater regret and sorrow to her royal father than several losses sustained by him before, as this beloved Royal, amiable daughter was brought up almost by the hands of His Majesty himself; since she was aged only 4 to 5 months, His Majesty has carried her to and fro by his hand and on the lap and placed her by his side in every one of the Royal seats, where ever he went; whatever could be done in the way of nursing His Majesty has done himself, by feeding her with milk obtained from her nurse, and sometimes with the milk of the cow, goat &c. poured in a teacup from which His Majesty fed her by means of a spoon, so this Royal daughter was as familiar with her father in her infancy as with her nurses.

On her being only aged six months, his Majesty took this princess with him and went to Ayudia on affairs there; after that time when she became grown up His Majesty had the princess seated on his lap when he was in his chair at the breakfast, dinner & supper table, and fed her at the same time of breakfast &c. almost every day, except when she became sick of colds &c. until the last days of her life she always eat at same table with her father. Where ever His Majesty went, this princess always accompanied her father upon the same, sedan, carriage, Royal boat, yacht &c. and on her being grown up she became more prudent than other children of the same age, she paid every affectionate attention to her affectionate and esteemed father in every thing where her ability was allowed; she was well educated in the vernacular Siamese literature, which she commenced to study when she was 3 years old, and in last year she commenced to study in the English School where the schoolmistress, Lady _____ has observed that she was more skillful than the other royal Children, she pronounced & spoke English in articulate & clever manner which pleased the schoolmistress exceedingly, so that the schoolmistress on the loss of this her beloved pupil, was in great sorrow and wept much.

. . . But alas! her life was very short. She was only aged 8 years & 20 days, reckoning from her birth day & hour, she lived in this world 2942 days & 18 hours. But it is known that the nature of human lives is like the flames of candles lighted in open air without any protection above & every side, so it is certain that this path ought to be followed by every one of human beings in a short or long while which cannot be ascertained by prediction, Alas!

Dated Royal Grand Palace, Bangkok
16th May, Anno Christi 1863

It was the custom for the royal family to retreat each June to the Summer Palace, a compound of buildings with red-lacquered roofs nestled among swaying palms overlooking the Andaman Sea. Once a joyful retreat, it had over the years grown neglected, its pavilions and wats home to shrieking gibbons and wild peafowl, the walls of the royal residence overgrown with vines. When Anna arrived there several weeks after Princess Fa-Ying's death, the entire compound had an air of such utter desolation that she wept well into the night. It was only Louis's worried voice that brought her back to earth once more.

She woke the next day determined to reclaim some sense of joy and order, both for herself and her students. Fa-Ying had not been the only child to die. By the time the cholera outbreak ended, several of the royal children had been buried, though none with so much ceremony as Fa-Ying. The events surrounding her funeral haunted Anna: the King's anguished face as the funeral urn was borne to the temple; the court musicians and monks whose voices were raised around the clock, offering prayers to hasten the child's soul from this world. Anna had thought she would go mad with grief, yet now that she was surrounded by only forest and a crescent beach, she thought she would go mad from the silence. She engaged Moonshee and Beebe in cleaning a beachside pavilion, making it suitable for a temporary classroom, and on their third evening there, she joined a solemn parade of children in setting tiny luminaries adrift upon the waves to honor their dead sister.

Prince Chulalongkorn led them in a silent procession, carrying a single lit taper and accompanied by the mournful cries of seabirds wheeling overhead and the hushed sound of waves breaking upon the shore. The sun had already disappeared on the rim of the world; violet shadows stretched before them, and a few stars appeared in the twilit sky. More than once Anna started to ask Chulalongkorn where they were going, but his sombre expression stopped her.

When at last they reached the edge of the beach, Anna saw a number of lotus-blossoms on the sand. In the center of each was a tiny petal-shape candle.

Slowly, and still without speaking, the children stepped toward them, kneeling and with great care picking up the flowers. Prince Chulalongkorn alone remained standing, his taper a slender gold column held before his face. One by one the children stood, lotus blossoms cupped in their hands, and walked back to their brother. He in his turn bowed to each child, then dipped the taper to light the little candles within the lotus blooms. Anna watched, her throat tight, as the children turned and walked to the water's edge. There they stooped and one at a time, set the luminaries afloat upon the gentle waves; then stood back to watch as their offerings were borne out to sea. For a long time they remained thus, unspeaking, their eyes fixed on the glowing blossoms like so many fallen stars; until at last the lotus flowers disappeared from view.

Of the King she saw nothing. Or rather, the little she did see of him was too much—his impassive face as he sat upon the porch of the Summer Palace, a Buddhist text in his lap as he stared silently into the distance. Night fell and still he did not move; only the glowing ember of the cheroot in his hand would indicate that he was alive at all, and not another rigid statue, set to stand guard against the demons and *phi* of the forest.

But there was one night spirit he could not shut out forever. As evening fell, there was a muted tinkling of silver and crystal on the veranda behind him. Incensed, the King stood, slamming the book on a table and shouting as his servants scurried from the porch.

"Inside! I take all meals *inside!*"

"It's not their fault, Your Majesty."

He turned to see Anna standing at the bottom of the veranda steps. The royal children waited in an orderly line behind her, watching their father with mingled wariness and expectation.

"Being such a beautiful evening," she went on, "the children hoped you might join them for a sunset picnic."

The King regarded her coldly. "Mem, I will always remember your feelings for my daughter. And you shall never forget you are not here to teach King."

He started inside. "Your Majesty," Anna called softly, fighting to keep desperation from her voice. "The children miss you terribly."

The King reached the doorway, then stopped.

"You cannot shut out the world forever," said Anna. He turned, unwillingly, and looked at her.

191

"Believe me, Your Majesty, I've tried. When—when my husband died, I thought my heart would never heal. I could barely breathe. But Louis needed me. He was my salvation."

The King's gaze was hard. "And yet you still refuse to live."

Anna blinked. "I beg your pardon?"

"A mother. A teacher. A widow. But you are never just *woman*."

"That is not fair."

"In spite of all you say, Mem is not accepting passing of husband," the King replied. "It is why you so protect son, and why you devote all time to books and issues. And why you cannot accept gift!"

"Why are you doing this?" cried Anna.

He stared at her, head held high. "Because you lie even to yourself. So do not lecture me, Mem Leonowens, about living. You are not qualified."

He turned and walked inside, closing the doors tightly behind him.

Despite the shadow cast by the King's overwhelming grief, the solitude and desolate beauty of the Summer Palace still cast its spell. Mornings the children would gather in the classroom pavilion, and Anna would teach for those few hours before the midday sun became too intense. On some days, her mind adrift as she circled aimlessly around the room, checking the children's spelling, she might look outside and see the King wandering alone on the beach. But he did not raise his head to see her watching him, and no summons came for her to dine with him in his residence.

Her own quarters felt airless and bleak. It was a small European-style building that had been constructed a decade before but seemed the remnant of another century altogether, so derelict were its bricks and floor tiles, the roof leaking in corners so that Moonshee had to set pails everywhere when it rained. Beebe would serve afternoon tea, while Anna wilted in her stiff English clothes, fanning herself despairingly. She cast longing glances out at the beach, where Lady Thiang and the other *Chao Chom Manda* swam, their discarded sarongs on the sand like so many heaps of blossoms. They did this daily, all save Tuptim. More than once, Anna had found the lovesick concubine sitting alone in a garden alcove, reading her love letter for the thousandth time. But despite the schoolteacher's gentle warning, Tuptim kept to herself, save for Anna's morning classes. She always appeared for these, coming in earlier than the children and sitting by herself in the very last row. It was on one such morning that Tuptim busied herself with preparing the room for Mem Leonowens, putting out chalk and sorting through the children's textbooks.

It seemed to Tuptim—who, despite her heartache, always watched the schoolteacher with grave interest—that many things went unnoticed by Mem these past weeks. It might have merely been the heat, or the drowsy rhythm of the days. But the night came when even Anna succumbed to the desultory splendor of the beach.

She sat curled in the chair in her candlelit bedroom, schoolwork in her lap, her nightgown and cap sticking to her damp skin like linen bandages. Her eyes tracked dully over the same sentence, again and again. When she realized what she was doing, she sighed, rubbing her eyes, and stared at the tintype of her husband on the little nightstand beside her.

A mother. A teacher. A widow. But you are never just woman. *Because you are afraid . . .*

The papers fell from her lap as she stood and walked to the window. Outside, a full moon bathed the beach in silver, sparking off the water like wisps of flame. There was a smell of salt and the sweet fragrance of jasmine. Almost without thinking she stepped outside, the door shutting softly as she crossed the porch. Beneath her nightgown her flesh felt sticky and hot; she lifted the coarse fabric, gasping as the breeze touched her. Quickly, before she could change her mind, she pulled the gown over her head and let it fall, then walked the few yards to the beach. The sand was cool beneath her bare feet, the breeze cooler now as well where it slid across her bare skin. She reached the water's edge, the waves receding from her as though in a dream of lost paradise, but as the next swell approached, she walked in slowly, lowering herself until the water covered her shoulders, her head thrown back as she let the waves wash away loneliness and grief and longing.

ten

Far away in Bangkok, in the dim expanse of the Kralahome's office, Prince Chowfa stood before an old map of Siam and proudly explained his theory of the Burmese military incursion to the Kralahome and General Alak.

"We have been searching for our Burmese killers here, here, and here," he said, pointing. "Believing their supply line would only come through Chiang Mai. But no one has seen them there for weeks."

"Perhaps they're traveling at night," said the general, nodding thoughtfully.

"Or," interrupted Prince Chowfa, "their only purpose is to distract us from their real point of attack. Say, Three Pagoda Pass."

He indicated a mountain range south of Chiang

Mai, and on the same latitude as Bangkok. The Kralahome and General Alak exchanged looks. They glanced at the Kralahome's attendants, standing at attention near the door, then switched to speaking English for privacy's sake.

"Three Pagodas Pass?" The general raised an eyebrow. "To march an army through there would take months."

"Yes," countered Prince Chowfa, "and how long have we been searching up north?"

A moment passed while the ramifications of this sank in. Stunned, the Kralahome turned to the general. "Could this be possible?" he asked, incredulous.

"Possible? No . . . " The general rubbed his chin. "But it would be brilliant." He looked at Prince Chowfa. "Assemble your regiment at once."

Prince Chowfa waied deeply and backed out of the chamber. As he did so, General Alak called after him.

"Your Highness? You will make a fine general someday."

The Prince beamed at the compliment. "You once said Taksin marched into Burma the same way," he said, and left.

• • •

That morning the King rose, reaching for his spectacles in their customary place at his bedside. They were not there. And a thorough search—even enlisting the aid of Nikorn and Putoi—still fueled to discover them. It was not until after breakfast that the King heard rustling outside his window. He rose, puzzled; then looked out to see a face peering in at him. Gray-bearded, ridiculously solemn: a monkey, wearing the King's spectacles. Mongkut laughed—for the first time since his daughter's death—laughed and laughed, until the monkey fled back into the trees.

On their side of the beach, the royal children slept in a rustically simple house, its windows open to the night. One of its doors had been left open as well, and in the sand outside was a single set of footprints that could be traced backward to the King's residence. The man who had left the footprints moved silently through the moonlit dormitory, making his way carefully between the dozens of futons and clouds of mosquito netting. Now and then he would stoop to retrieve an errant doll or dropped toy, then stand once more and continue on his rounds, straightening the

199

netting above one child's head, smoothing another's brow, bending to kiss the cheek of yet another. He continued thus until the night had paled to lavender and the first birds began crying in the forest. Finally he turned and quietly departed, leaving another set of footprints to mingle with the first in the sand outside.

In front of her own summer retreat, Anna sat at water's edge, unbound hair hanging heavily on her neck, a lantern on the sand beside her. The warm tropical wind carried with it the scents of night-blooming jasmine and wild ginger, and overhead the moon glowed lavender-white, another exotic bloom. She was leaning forward, tentatively untying the crosshatch of lace on her nightgown, when something stirred behind her.

"These hours are meant for sleep, Mem."

Anna spun around, clutching her nightgown. A few yards away, the King sat on a rock overlooking the beach, smoking a cheroot.

"You—you startled me."

"I thought it wise to do so."

Their eyes met, too briefly, as the shadow left by their last conversation enveloped them. "Might I ask what His Majesty is doing awake at such an ungodly hour?"

The King smiled ruefully, tilting his head to stare at the sky. "Gazing at the moon."

Anna let her head fall back and took in the sweep of unclouded sky, the darkness washed to the color of a mussel shell by the moonlight. "She's beautiful," she said softly.

The King nodded. "As the sun rises, she will surrender the night," he said dreamily. "But she is always with him . . . even when he cannot see her."

Anna listened, not daring to let herself turn and look at him. After a moment she said, "It must be a great comfort to him."

"Yes."

The King stood, and Anna moved aside so that he could sit down beside her. "This come from Bangkok," he said, holding out a letter. "You might find it of some interest."

She took the letter and began to read, then looked up in surprise.

"It's from—"

The King nodded. "Yes, please to read aloud," he urged. "As monkeys have stolen King's glasses."

She looked down and cleared her throat.

"'Your Majesty,'" she read. "'The United States sincerely appreciates your generous offer to help end this tragic conflict. Unfortunately, our country does not reach a latitude which favors the elephant. We are, however, highly grateful for this indication of friendship. Your good friend . . . '"

Anna looked up, touched. "'Abraham Lincoln.'"

The King glanced out across the moonlit ocean. He hesitated, then turned back to Anna, speaking with some difficulty. "I have always admired this man for what he is trying to do for his people. They say at the Battle of Antietam seventy thousand men killed each other in one day."

Anna listened with compassion as the King continued. "Each one of those soldiers had a father who grieves . . ."

"I am father to all of Siam. Mem not wrong about moving on."

Anna held his gaze. "Neither were you, Your Majesty."

"When we return to palace, it is time for teacher to teach Chulalongkorn and others any subject she wish—as long as King know first, so he can be prepared for consequences."

"I shall do my best, Your Majesty."

He stood and walked back toward the Summer Palace. Anna watched him go, biting her lip as she thought of her own apology. Suddenly the King stopped, turned, and stared back at her.

"And I was always believing English women slept in hats," he called, raising a hand in farewell.

Anna blushed as he disappeared into the night.

It took Prince Chowfa's men three days to reach the mountain pass, using cannon-mounted elephant and horse, riding through the night and stopping only to rest their mounts and eat sparingly. On the morning of the fourth day one of their scouts returned at a gallop. He reined in his horse as he approached Prince Chowfa and the general, riding atop elephants and surrounded by a small regiment of mounted and ground troops.

"Burmese, General, just over that ridge," he called breathlessly. "I can't tell how many of them . . ."

The General nodded at Prince Chowfa. "Congratulations on your foresight. Let us begin to bring it to fruition."

They dismounted, calling out orders to their men, then followed as the troops descended on the enemy.

The base camp was within the ruins of an ancient temple, well hidden by the shadows of the mountain ridge. But even in the dimness Chowfa could make out the guerrilla squadron: an impressive assemblage of ruthless, unsavory-looking fighting men. They were busy cleaning weapons, cooking food over a small, smoky campfire, and drinking from a cask of wine. Other casks were strewn about, seemingly empty.

"Now?" whispered the Prince.

The General nodded. "Now."

Gunshots rang out as General Alak's soldiers swarmed over the camp. Several Burmese soldiers fell as the rest, panicked, grabbed what they could and scattered across the ruins and into the woods.

"That was easy enough." General Alak motioned to Prince Chowfa. The two of them strolled into the clearing, stopping when they reached a campfire laid in the ruins of an ancient palace. The general leaned down to pick up a ladle, dipped it into a cast-iron cookpot, and sniffed appreciatively. "Let us hope they are better cooks than they are soldiers." He raised a hand and shouted to his men, "We stay here tonight!"

The men laughed and began to make themselves at home. In twos and threes, the rest of the regiment returned, bearing news of the guerrillas' ignominious retreat. Prince Chowfa felt light-headed with pride. As he sat with the men a short while later, feasting on the spoils, he imagined his brother's face when he received news of their victory. His pleasure at the triumph, the questions he would have afterward, during the inevitable postmortem, when he would question his brother about every detail of the battle . . .

Prince Chowfa frowned.

In the darkness, General Alak was making yet another circuit of the camp. Behind were his lieutenants, carrying a flask of wine and refilling the soldiers' glasses. When he reached Prince Chowfa, the general extended a hand for the younger man's goblet.

"You should be celebrating," he said with a smile. "Your country owes you a debt of gratitude. Your instincts were excellent."

The Prince looked at him, troubled. "They ran off too easily."

"Nonsense." Alak scuffled around in the underbrush until he found an empty glass, then poured himself some wine.

"To His Majesty and the greatness of Siam," he announced. His lieutenants raised their glasses and drank. The general held his goblet, waiting for Prince Chowfa to join in.

But the Prince did not. Instead he sat and for a long moment regarded the general warily.

Alak's eyes narrowed. "You would not drink to your own brother?"

"You said my instincts were good."

The general tilted his head. "And what are they telling you?"

"That you're not drinking, either."

As at a signal, the clearing grew quiet. Then a terrible sound came from the darkness, softly at first, growing louder with each passing second—the low, urgent noise of a man vomiting. After a moment the noise had an echo, and another, and another; urgency and terror grew, until the entire clearing was wracked by anguished groans and the dull thud of bodies dropping. Horrified, the young Prince gazed at General Alak, his expression rent by despair as he realized the depth of his hero's betrayal. Around them the four Lieutenants stared at them in confusion, until one suddenly doubled over, vomiting blood.

"Sir." He gasped. Beside him the others sank to their knees, moaning. "Please . . ."

Prince Chowfa bolted. With a cry, General Alak snatched a pistol from one of the dying men and raced after him. The terrifed Prince sprinted past his dying troops toward the building's steps. He tried to grab a weapon, but the general was only yards behind when he reached the bottom of the broad stairs. Prince Chowfa raced up them, turned, and ran frantically down a long, broken colonnade, leaping over fallen mortar as the general rapidly closed in behind him. When he came to the end of the colonnade, chips of mortar exploded from the arch overhead as the general fired at him. There was a balcony there, overlooking the woods below. Desperately the Prince leaped, hitting the ground and rolling as he tried to regain his balance.

But it was too much. He groaned aloud: the fall had shattered his leg. Still he tried to run, hobbling pathetically toward the trees as the sound of General Alak's footsteps grew louder and louder behind him.

In the darkness something loomed. Prince Chowfa tried to turn aside, instead found himself stumbling headlong into a huge tree. Dazed, he stumbled backward and fell. As he did so, General Alak appeared, circling him calmly.

"My mercenaries needed uniforms," he said, glancing back at the mass of fallen men, some still moaning as they struggled to crawl from the clearing.

Prince Chowfa gasped. "You killed your own regiment?"

"Yes. In war innocent people die, but only a war will cleanse this nation of its Western parasites."

He raised his pistol, aiming it at the Prince's head.

"Take comfort, Chowfa. Your family will soon be joining you . . ."

A single gunshot rang out, its echoes splintering across the forest. But except for the man standing triumphantly above the bloodstained body of the Prince, there was no one left alive to hear it.

"Mem, there is a messenger from the King's house outside with invitation for you."

Anna looked up from her breakfast: fruits gathered from a stand of trees by the beach, steamed rice, and fish just caught that morning. "From the King?"

Beebe shrugged, gesturing at the door, and smiled. "It *is* a beautiful morning, Mem. Even a king may be stirred by such a day."

Anna nodded. "Well, then. I don't suppose I'll have the opportunity to finish this splendid meal. But thank you, Beebe."

She walked outside, where a servant bowed and

recited carefully, "King wishes Mem and son join him and royal children at sea."

Anna looked puzzled. The servant frowned, then motioned at the beach. "Sea . . . ?"

"At the beach, you mean?"

The servant smiled.

Anna thanked him graciously, and he left. For a moment she stood outside, letting the cool breeze lift her hair and the sun warm her arms. It *was* a beautiful day, the air clear as water. In the near distance the waves moved back and forth across the sand as slowly as though drawn by invisible hands. *Like someone making a bed*, Anna thought, and blushed. Then, laughing for pure delight, she turned and ran into the house.

"Louis! Get dressed, Louis! We're going out!"

An hour later, they met the King and his entourage on the beach. Servants held dozens of horses, the animals snorting and tossing their heads as they chafed to run. King Mongkut sat astride his magnificent black stallion, its saddle agleam with gold and scarlet tassles. Beside him, a chestnut horse waited for Anna to mount. She did so breathlessly—how long had it been since she'd ridden? Years, it seemed—and watched as Prince Chu-

209

lalongkorn and Louis and the royal children mounted, the smaller ones seated two and three to a pony, the wives and concubines riding behind them with more bodyguards on horseback. For a moment when everyone was mounted and each horse seemed frozen, it presented a brilliant tableau of toy horses and toy children and women tossed across the beach, all looking to where a toy King, resplendent in black and crimson, sat upon a beautiful toy horse. Then with a cry the King spurred his mount. The black stallion reared, then cantered into the surf. With squeals and shouts of delight, the entire entourage gave chase.

They rode for an hour, following the coast as it wound past forests and lagoons, ruins and waterfalls, until at last they reached Cape Clegg. Here they dismounted. In the distance mountains reared above the forest and the sun fell golden upon its emerald slopes, but nearby a grove of stately trees provided shade. Butterflies flitted in and out between them, and in the upper branches a hornbill sat, rattling its beak defensively.

"It's so beautiful," breathed Anna, and the King smiled.

Servants hurried to set up tables for lunch. The

children leaped from their horses, the older ones racing after Louis to arrange a game of croquet. Others ran down to the beach to fly the small diamond-shaped fighter kites called *pukpao*, or hunt for shells in the sand. Anna dismounted, gratefully taking a drink handed to her by a servant, then walked over to where the croquet game was getting under way.

"Mem! Will you play on our team?" cried Prince Chulalongkorn.

"And, Father—you on ours!"

Anna laughed and bowed to the Prince. "I accept your invitation, Your Highness."

"And I yours," the King said solemnly, bowing to one of his daughters, then grabbing her in a hug.

The game was leisurely, the children easily distracted by a circle of brilliant red mushrooms sprouting near one wicket, a nest of glowworm larvae beneath another. Butterflies flew among the laughing group, and once a macaque peered down from an overhanging tree, then scampered off chattering when Prince Chulalongkorn tried to climb after it. Anna and King Mongkut waited patiently as the children played, sipping cool fruit drinks and fanning themselves with leaves.

"I look at them, Mem, and feel such hope," said

the King. He leaned on his croquet mallet, a smile creasing his face as he watched the Prince dangling from a branch. "Why is it only in children that we see such human potential?"

Anna nodded. It was not a question that needed an answer. For some minutes they stood in companionable silence, waving when one of the children called out excitedly and laughing when Chulalongkorn tumbled into the grass. Anna smiled, brushing the hair from her eyes, then turned to the King. Her voice was low, her expression thoughtful, almost grave.

"Thank you for bringing me here, Your Majesty. To Siam, I mean . . ."

She gestured at the grove full of children, the mountains shining in the distance. "I would hate to think where Louis and I might be if your letter hadn't arrived when it did."

"Were you happy in Bombay?"

Anna considered for a moment. "I was never unhappy," she said slowly. "But to tell you the truth, I don't think I ever quite fit in, either."

The King looked at her in surprise. "A woman like you? How could it be so?"

"I suppose it's because my whole life seems to be

one long quest to belong somewhere. I left England as a child—my husband left me in Bombay and now I find myself here, with you . . . wondering where I fit in exactly."

The King listened, then nodded. "Your path is as it should be."

Anna blushed. "My mind has sent me down several roads in recent days, Your Majesty—all of which lead absolutely nowhere." She smiled ruefully. "What would Buddha say of that?"

"That roads are for journeys, Mem, not destinations."

A ball came careening through the grass, settling at Anna's feet. She looked down and took aim, handling her mallet expertly, and sent her own ball rocketing straight for the King's. With a hollow *thwack*, his went flying. Anna kept herself from smiling but instead looked over at the King through a fringe of windblown hair, and asked, "Don't your wives ever get jealous?"

King Mongkut frowned. "I do not understand significance of question."

"I'm prying. Forgive me."

The King leaned on his mallet. "No, please. Continue."

"Most of the world believes a man and woman should have a relationship which is sacred unto them."

"Each of my wives believes same about King," Mongkut replied matter-of-factly.

Anna hesitated. "Not everyone can marry you, Your Majesty," she said.

"Good thing, too. King needs his rest sometime."

Anna turned bright crimson. The King chuckled, and she said, "I could never imagine sharing my husband with anyone."

"Why not?"

"Because . . . he's mine."

"Ha! Like slave."

"No!" Then, laughing, she added, "Well, perhaps, but strictly a voluntary one."

The King shook his head in mock dismay. "A man becomes slave to woman, and they call *my* country uncivilized."

Grinning, Anna turned and smartly knocked the King's croquet ball so that it went spinning out of sight. His eyes narrowed, and he said playfully, "King's wives often let King win."

Anna laughed. "Then *I* won't have to, will I?"

The children's laughter joined them on the

breeze as the two of them turned, smiling, and walked across the field.

The picnic at Cape Clegg was a turning point in the summer. The royal family was a family again, albeit a large one.

And Anna—somewhat warily, it must be allowed—felt herself a part of that immense and complicated organism. Every morning the lessons proceeded smoothly, but for a shorter length of time, and the rest of the day was given over to games or expeditions into the forest to collect iridescent beetles and feathers, fruiting ginger, and lizards who regarded their captors with unnaturally calm, gold-flecked eyes.

The servants were kept busy with the ongoing search for the King's spectacles. Anna had thought His Majesty was joking when he said that monkeys had taken them, but more than once she herself had seen the monkey in question, a rather imposing male who wore them on top of his head and managed, improbably, to keep from losing them as he leapt and chattered among his clan. Very early each morning, while the King knelt outside his private temple making his daily prayers, two servants assigned specifically to the task set about trying to lure the monkey thief from his tree. They used bananas as bait, dangling from the end of a long stick, but every day the men admitted defeat, as the monkey cackled at them triumphantly from his perch.

This morning began no differently. King Mongkut knelt in his customary place, the vast golden Buddha looming above him like the sun itself, resplendent in the dawn. He lit a joss stick and began his morning prayers.

"Phutho di chai chak nak n' chai nak na . . ."

The sound of his chanting rose and mingled with the frustrated voices of the servants as they followed the monkey from tree to tree. The spectacles glittered from his head, and he seemed to leer down at them.

Then one of the men positioned himself so that he could lift the heavy bunch of bananas, dangling it directly in front of the monkey's face. The animal grew silent, then slowly extended one long-fingered hand toward the fruit. A second servant crept behind him, his hand reaching for the spectacles, but at the last moment the monkey snatched the bananas and sprang off, shrieking gleefully as he swung from limb to limb, heading down toward the beach.

The men gave chase, stumbling through the underbrush as they approached the sand. Suddenly one stopped.

"*Mai di . . .*"

Hand trembling, he pointed. Concealed beneath a pile of palm fronds, something gleamed in the shadows—the bow of a small canoe, ornately carved in the Burmese style. The two men turned to each other, their hunt forgotten, then began sprinting toward the King's residence.

But when they arrived, the King was no longer alone. His bodyguard stood a few yards away, hesitant even now to interrupt the King at his prayers; but he knew his master's peace was to be shattered now, perhaps forever.

"Your Majesty." Nikorn hesitated, then said, "The Kralahome has arrived at last from the capital. He has—he has news."

"Bring him here immediately."

The Kralahome had not even to speak for the King to know to nature of his news: his anguished face was enough. He knelt before the King, struggling to keep his voice steady as he recounted the massacre of Prince Chowfa, General Alak, and their regiment.

". . . The villagers said all the bodies had been stripped and left to the sun. I fear Prince Chowfa and Alak were cremated with the others."

The King stared into the trees, devastated. "May their souls rest in peace," he murmured, motioning for the Kralahome to rise. "And may my brother forgive me for doubting him."

For a long moment the men stood in the sunlight outside the temple, silent. At last the Kralahome spoke.

"You could not have prevented your brother's death, Your Majesty."

The King said nothing, only stood with eyes closed, his hands at his side. He seemed to have returned to his mediation, but after some minutes had passed he opened his eyes.

"Send the armies to every province along our Burmese border and tell their emissary that we are preparing for war. Inform the servants that we are returning to the capital. And tell Mrs. Leonowens that I wish to see her—immediately."

eleven

It was an hour before Anna arrived, escorted by Nikorn. She was out of breath and barefoot, carrying a fishing net full of seashells.

"I'm terribly sorry, Your Majesty," she said. "I had no idea you were looking for me. I went clear around the cove . . ."

The King sat in a simple chair at the window of his study, staring out at the distant mountains. For a long moment he did not answer. Finally he turned to her.

"I have been wondering, Mem. When it is my son's turn to become King, will he be a good one?"

Anna felt a chill at the King's words and somber demeanor. "Why? What has happened?"

"Please." The King gestured at her imploringly. Anna hesitated, setting down her shells, then ran a hand through her hair and stepped toward him.

"Well, he is keenly intelligent, with a warm heart and a sympathetic soul. Qualities, I think, of a great king. Yet there's still so much for him to learn—so much he is eager to learn."

The King stared at her, lost in thought. At last he said, "Mem, how would you answer question about Prince's ability to rule if he had to become king now?"

"He is still a boy." Anna bit her lip, then asked apprehensively, "Please, tell me what has happened."

The King held her look. Then he stood, crossing the room to a small alcove where candles were arranged between pretty stones and a conch shell one of the children had brought him. Shadows lengthened behind him as he began lighting the tapers.

"This morning a Burmese boat was discovered on the beach. Then the Kralahome arrived himself to tell me that the regiment led by General Alak and my brother was ambushed near the border. There were no survivors."

Anna paled. The King lit the last taper and turned to face her. It was a moment before she could speak.

"I—how can you be so calm?" she asked.

"Which is why," the King went on, "I must know about son, so he may ascend throne whenever my time comes."

Anna swallowed. "Your—your son will make an excellent king, Your Majesty."

The King was silent. At last he nodded, as though this was the answer he had been hoping for. "Then he must prepare for noviciation ceremony. To understand he is great, since he is part of the Infinite, but great in that one thing alone."

"How does a twelve-year-old boy do that?" Anna's voice broke, but she would not look away. The King gazed back at her, the candles casting a glow over the twilit chamber. They remained thus for a long, long time, silent, bodies separated by the smoke-fragrant air between them, their hearts and minds held in sway by the unanswered, unanswerable question that bound them.

Anna had never witnessed anything as beautiful or solemn as Prince Chulalongkorn's noviciation. The Temple of the Emerald Buddha was opened for the ceremony, and hundreds of monks filled it, chanting as the King stood above his son. The boy's head was bowed, eyes closed, as his father anointed him with lustral water from a conch shell. His head and his eyebrows had been shaved, the opulent trappings of a crown prince discarded for the simple white robes of a novitiate. Just as his father had done decades before, Chulalongkorn was entering the brotherhood of Buddhist monks. Henceforth he would receive his food by begging with a wooden bowl; henceforth he would own nothing more than that bowl, and his robes, and a pair of sandals.

Until the day came that he himself stood within the Temple of the Emerald Buddha and received the burden of the kingship of Siam.

"Thou who art come out of the pure waters, be thy offenses washed away, bear in this bosom the brightness of light which shall lead thee at once and forever . . ."

The King turned and presented an alms bowl to the abbot, who then plced the sling of the bowl over the Prince's head.

"Phutho di chai nak n'! Chai nak na!" the monks chanted. *Merciful Buddha, we are joyous indeed . . .*

Chulalongkorn stood, his father beside him. Together they lifted their faces to the calm gaze of the Emerald Buddha and smiled.

• • •

When the Prince's ceremony was finished, the King and his retinue departed, followed by the abbot and the other monks, the new novitiate among them. Outside, the King turned right, back toward the Grand Palace; Chulalongkorn and the others left, to their spartan home in a neighboring temple. As the monks filed off, a single figure lingered, a monk clad as the others were in saffron robes and wooden sandals, shaven head bowed. It was only when he passed the gate leading to the Palace that Balat stopped. He stood as long as he dared, looking around hopefully for some sign of Tuptim, but she was nowhere to be seen.

Anna found Sunday services at the Bangkok Anglican Church to be somewhat less impressive than Prince Chulalongkorn's noviciation. She sat, sweltering, in the last pew, the words in the hymnal before her blurring as she joined the rest of the congregation in singing "Onward, Christian Soldiers." When the service was finally over, she hurried outside, waiting as the other members of the city's English colony streamed past the minister, shaking his hand and murmuring pleasantries. Only when the English congregation walked down the steps and onto the street did they note with concern the Siamese Offensive Expedition, led by five regally uniformed noblemen, marching past.

"Lord Bradley!" Anna edged her way through the crowd, waving. "Lady Bradley, Mr. Kincaid . . ."

Lord Bradley shaded his eyes with a missal and smiled at the younger woman. "Madam Leonowens! How nice to see you out in the real world! My wife and I were just speaking of you—will you join us for tea?"

"Yes. Certainly."

She followed them to their carriage, making small talk and doing the best she could to restrain herself from springing her questions upon Lord Bradley. There were perhaps a dozen others at the Bradleys when they arrived, all members of the city's English community, and Anna joined them upon the veranda, where they safely watched the continuing parade of Siamese soldiers long into the afternoon. Throughout the house servants were busy packing, moving cartons and suitcases as their masters talked in tones alternately calm and alarmed about the recent massacre along the border. Tea had been served and gossip exchanged, and the first visitors were readying themselves to leave, when Anna finally approached her hosts.

"Lord Bradley, Lady Bradley. Mr. Kincaid." She nodded at all three respectfully. "If I could have a moment of your time."

Lord Bradley nodded. "I'm afraid, Mrs. Leonowens, a moment is all we have."

"We're leaving on the next boat, my dear," added Lady Bradley. "And so should you."

"My life is here, Lady Bradley."

Kincaid shook his head. "Nasty business, all this saber rattling. Not good for trade, I can tell you."

"The King's brother is dead, Mr. Kincaid, along with his general." Anna's eyes flashed as she turned to the ruddy-faced businessman. "I would hardly call this action unprovoked."

Lord Bradley stepped between them. "What can I do for you, Mrs. Leonowens?" he asked, his tone condescending.

"Answer a question, if you would. Are the British behind these attacks on Siam?"

Kincaid snickered. "Stick to teaching, Mrs. Leonowens. It's obvious you know nothing about politics."

Anna went on, undeterred. "Burma would not dare make a move without England's blessing."

"Precisely." Lord Bradley turned to gaze down at the street, where yet another battalion of gorgeously uniformed Siamese was marching past. "But if this crisis isn't resolved soon, and a country under our protection is threatened, we will have no choice but to defend our interests."

"*Our* protection,'" repeated Anna angrily. "'*Our* interests.'"

"The ways of England are the ways of the world, my dear," said Lady Bradley.

"They are the ways of one world, Lady Bradley— one I'm ashamed to call my own."

Lord Bradley looked her up and down coldly. "You forget yourself, madam. Now, if you'll excuse us . . ."

He turned to his wife. She took his arm, and they started for the stairs.

"No, sir, I will not!" The other guests turned as Anna's voice rang out angrily across the terrace. "You raised a glass to him, you commended him for his vision, but all the while you are waiting to take his country away from him."

Lord Bradley stopped and stared at her haughtily. "How the empire conducts its business is really none of your concern."

"Last time I checked, Lord Bradley, I was still a British subject."

"A fact you would do well to remember, madam, next time you're cheek-to-cheek with the King."

And the Bradleys swept off down the stairs, leaving Anna standing red-faced and furious among the few remaining English guests.

She returned home, her anger and embarrassment burned away by exhaustion. The excitement seemed to have tired out everyone. Louis had already gone to sleep, tucked in by Beebe, and so Anna, too, prepared for bed early, adjusting the flame of an oil lamp so that it cast a warm glow across the room. She was just settling in when she heard something move across the room.

"Who is it?" she cried.

On the far side of her bedchamber a young woman stood in the pool of golden lamplight. Her hands were raised, and there was a dagger thrust in her belt, but when Anna opened her mouth to shout for help the girl *wai*ed deeply, dropping to her knees.

"Please," she whispered. "No one must see me! I am Phim. My Lady Tuptim needs you."

Without a word Anna grabbed a batiked shawl, cov-

227

ered her head, and gestured at the back door. "Go then," she commanded in a low voice. "Bring me to her."

The girl led her past the river and toward a part of the city where Anna had never been, following a narrow path that wound alongside the *klong*. The smell of rotting fish was so strong that Anna pulled the scarf over her mouth and nose, but still she hurried silently after Phim. They crossed an empty square behind a Chinese temple, Phim looking around furtively as she darted ahead of Anna into an alley barely wide enough to hold her. At the mouth of the alley Anna hesitated; she could see Phim a few feet away, shrouded in shadow, one hand on her dagger.

"What is it?" Anna whispered, poised to run.

Phim pressed herself against the wall. From the darkness behind her another figure appeared, passing the young girl and stepping out into the square. A slender figure with a shaved head and eyebrows, wearing the saffron robes of a Buddhist monk.

Tuptim.

Anna gasped. "Dear girl, what have you done?"

Tuptim approached her, hand outstretched. "What I have done is not result of King or intention to dishonor. A concubine's heart is of no consequence to man consumed with matters of whole universe."

Anna shook her head in dismay. "Tuptim, *why*? Why didn't you come to me? The King might have understood. How could you do this to him?"

"If love was a choice, who would ever choose such exquisite pain? This is what I need His Majesty to know, if such does not compromise Mem."

"I will tell the King anything you wish, but—"

Tuptim smiled. "I thank Buddha for giving me direction, and now, with Mem before me, I thank him for giving me true friend."

Light filled the square, and the sound of footsteps.

"We were followed!" cried Phim.

Across the open space palace guards were running, lanterns held high. At the sight of the three women they called out excitedly and raced toward them. Anna stared, stunned, then turned and ran after Tuptim and Phim.

Anna escaped—or rather, she was apprehended and immediately released. Tuptim and Phim were not.

Two days passed. Each morning Anna presented herself at the door of the Kralahome's rooftop suite;

each morning he failed to appear. It was not until the third day, as somber nobles leaned on the balustrade and spoke in low, urgent voices, that the Prime Minister arrived, flanked by several other men.

"Your Excellency."

Anna stopped pacing and ran to meet him. The Kralahome ignored her, continuing until he reached the steps. When Anna tried to follow, he snapped, "King cannot see you now."

"In light of the situation, that is unacceptable."

"In light of more critical situation, sir, it is as it shall be."

"Where is Tuptim?" Anna cried. "What crime is she being charged with?"

The Kralahome stopped at the bottom step, turned, and regarded her spitefully. "Her fate is none of your concern."

In fact, it was a simple matter to locate Tuptim. She was being held in the prison within the royal palace grounds. Her trial was to commence immediately. Anna scarcely had time to go home and get Moonshee to serve as both escort and moral support. She entered the Hall of Justice warily, but her trepidation turned at once to genuine dread. The chamber had none of the comfort or beauty she had come to associate with Bangkok: it was a large, sparely furnished chamber, crowded with members of the royal household. A tribunal of judges, both men and women, sat in tiered rows to one side. The magistrate, Justice Phya Phrom, a hard-faced man in his fifties, commanded the center of a platform overlooking the chamber. The gallery was packed with onlookers, many of them haughty dowagers, and Anna's heart sank when she recognized the cruel features of Lady Jao Jom Manda Ung in the first row.

"Pay no attention, memsahib," whispered Moonshee as Lady Jao Jom cast a withering look at Anna. "Come, we must sit."

They found a seat at the back of the room, and had no sooner settled down when a gong sounded. The room fell silent. Moonshee's hand tightened around Anna's as a side door opened, and a slow procession emerged.

Anna gasped. So did everyone else, as a quartet of brutish-looking guards led a slight figure before the magistrate. Gaunt-faced, her beauty now that of a skull, all bone and hollow, staring eyes. Her hands and feet were chained, and Anna wondered, sick at heart, how the chains were able to constrain her—she was so thin, it seemed her limbs could slide through like water. The guards dragged her to the defendant stand and thrust her there, pushing her to her knees. Tuptim's head sank, but then she lifted it and looked around the room, until her gaze found Anna's. The two women stared at each other for a long moment, until one of the guards yanked the prisoner's chain and shouted a command in Siamese. Tuptim sprawled on the ground, and Anna turned to see the last guard laying several items before the magistrate—a cowled robe, the novice's vestments known as *nens*, and a yellow silken envelope: an amulet.

Another gong echoed through the room. The magistrate raised his head and in a thundering voice proclaimed, "Khun Jao Tuptim, you are accused of a traitorous act against His Majesty, King Mongkut, which carries the penalty of death."

In the defendant's dock, Tuptim got to her feet and stood. Anna squeezed Moonshee's hand, as Lady Jao Jom Manda Ung's thin lips pursed in a small smile and the other dowagers nodded approvingly. Hastily the magistrate cast a sharp glance at them, and they looked down.

"Please describe for the court the events as they occurred," he ordered Tuptim.

Tuptim gazed at him, her gaze respectful yet unafraid. "Why say anything if I am not to be judged fairly?"

The judges stiffened at what they saw as insolence. Justice Phya Phrom studied her, then signaled the bailiff, who turned and quickly walked to the rear of the court and opened the door. Two guards entered, carrying a litter. The chamber erupted into gasps and soft cries as everyone recognized the naked form of a young priest, his torso contorted and bloodied with the marks of torture. On the defendant's stand, Tuptim swayed, her entire body shaking as she gazed upon her beloved. Anna shut her eyes, then forced herself to open them again as the justice's voice boomed.

"Is this not the priest whose letter was found in your chamber, written in English—no doubt to disguise its lascivious intent—?"

The bailiff picked up the yellow silken amulet, opened it, and handed a slip of paper to the justice. He read the name inscribed there.

"—Khun Phra Balat?"

He handed the paper back to the bailiff, who

passed it to the other judges. They examined it, murmuring. Tuptim's eyes remained riveted upon Balat's twisted form, and Anna leaned forward, holding her breath as she sought to hear the young man's weak voice speaking in English.

"Fear not, Tuptim . . . all life is suffering . . ."

Justice Phya Phrom looked up, made a slashing motion. A guard stooped and backhanded the priest. Tears coursed down Tuptim's face as the justice commanded, "Speak now, woman, or the cane shall be applied to you at once."

Anna watched as Tuptim drew a deep, shuddering breath. Without taking her eyes from Balat, she began to speak, her voice trembling.

"My lords, Khun Phra Balat is the only man I have ever loved, and being taken from him was to deny air to my lungs. The King does not *need* me"—she pointed at Balat—"but I need *him!* So much so, I am convinced it was Buddha who guided my actions."

Muttered voices rose angrily throughout the room. One of the judges cried, "Buddha would not fill your head with such wickedness!"

Tuptim drew her head up and went on. "He wrote to me to bid me farewell, believing I was now forever *nang ham*, a forbidden woman, and lost forever in the *Khang nai*. He said he would never marry another woman, and so committed his life to a monastery . . ."

Blood pounded in Anna's ears as she recalled the envelope she had given the girl. *Oh, Tuptim! How could I . . . ?*

Another one of the judges stooped to pick up the yellow monk's *nens* and demanded insistently, "So he disguised you as the most sacred of human beings so that you could consummate this—this—"

"No! No, he did nothing!" Tuptim cried. "I disguised myself. I joined a procession leaving the palace—when I knew he could not recognize me—and I became one of his brothers."

There were cries of outraged disbelief from the dowagers as Judge Phya Phrom and his colleagues regarded Tuptim with incredulous amusement.

"I speak the truth!" she said desperately. She turned, searching the courtroom until she found Anna, and pointed. "Mem Anna is here, she will tell you!"

Anna hesitated, unsure of courtroom protocol, then began to stand. But before she could do so, Justice Phya Phrom declaimed, in English, "Mem Leonowens has no voice here."

Anna shrank back into her seat. In the gallery facing her, Lady Jao Jom smiled in triumph. The justice turned back to Tuptim.

"You have denigrated King Mongkut and Lord Buddha. You have defiled a monastery with your female presence, and destroyed this monk's vow of celibacy."

"He never knew I was a woman!"

"He gave you the robe and you went to his bed!" Justice Phya Phrom shouted.

"That is not true, and I condemn you for your foul thoughts and cruel hearts!"

Her brave retort echoed through the room like a thunderbolt. As its echoes faded, the only sound was the scratching of scribes transcribing her words. Finally Justice Phya Phrom shook his head.

"Khun Jao Tuptim, in not confessing, you too are bringing upon yourself many agonies that will come before your death."

Tuptim stood, silent, in the dock. She lifted her chained hands and crossed them upon her breast. Her eyes never left Balat.

Justice Phya Phro turned and motioned to the guards. "Begin."

Feeling as though she were in some frozen nightmare, Anna watched, powerless, as the guards stepped forward. Silently and relentlessly they tore the prisoner's clothes from her, stripping her from the waist up. Then they grabbed her and threw her onto the litter beside Balat. Lady Jao Jom and the other dowagers rose in anticipation as the guards raised their bastinados and, as one, brought them down upon the girl's naked shoulders.

Tuptim screamed, once, then doubled over with the effort of swallowing her cries. Long red welts bloomed across her back, opening as the bastinados fell again and again, and rivulets of blood streamed to the floor.

"Stop it!"

Heads turned as Anna sprang from her seat, shouting so loudly, her throat ached. "Do you hear me? Don't you dare lay another hand on her!"

Moonshee watched, speechless, as Anna pushed through the gallery toward Tuptim, past the sputtering Lady Jao Jom and other dowagers. But before she could reach Tuptim, the guards grabbed her. Anna struggled

237

with them, turning to shout at Justice Phya Phrom.

"She has done nothing but try to find happiness! Don't touch me!" She kicked savagely at a guard, then went on, panting, "I am going straight to the King! He will put an end to this savagery!"

And as the courtroom looked on in amazement, the guards released her. With one last look at Tuptim, Anna turned and fled the chamber, Moonshee hurrying after her.

The King awaited her somberly in the deserted Audience Hall. It was the first time she had ever seen him there alone. For a moment unease almost overcame her outrage, but Anna took a deep breath and walked quickly toward the dais, her heels clattering loudly on the marble floor.

"Thank you for seeing me, Your Majesty," she said, curtsying. "The Prime Minister told me this was none of my concern—"

"It *is* none of Mem's concern," the King interrupted, "and King is seeing you now to tell you same himself."

"Forgive me, Your Majesty, but—"

"I do not wish for you to talk more on this, Mem. To King or anyone."

"I'm only trying to—"

"Tuptim broke law, madam! Now do as I say, and *go!*"

Anna stood frozen, staring at him with disbelief as he gazed back with stony eyes.

"Why are you behaving like this?" she asked in a low voice. "I know you have matters of tremendous importance weighing on you, but you are a man of honor, of compassion."

"She broke law."

"By loving someone?" Anna's voice rose as she went on deliberately. "Sacrifice your life for truth. Persecute no man. Govern yourself in thought, word, and deed. Are these not the teachings of Buddha?"

Mongkut started from his throne. "I am King and I say *enough!*"

His hand knocked against an adjoining table, sending a betel-nut tray flying. It crashed to the floor, porcelain shattering everywhere. Immediately his bodyguards were in the doorway, but at sight of their King's face they withdrew.

"You asked me to always tell you what I think."

His eyes held Anna's, unblinking, but his voice shook with emotion as he spoke. "What you think, and what you do, and how and when you do them,

239

are not the same thing. If you believe I wish to execute this girl—but now, because you say to court, 'Mem can tell King what to do,' I cannot intervene as I had planned!"

"Intervene?" broke in Anna. "*After* they're tortured?"

"Yes!" cried the King. "But you—a woman, and a foreigner—you have made it seem the King is at *your* command! You have made me appear weak, and now it is impossible for me to step in and not lose face!"

His words rang in the air between them. It was a moment before she realized what she had done. Then Anna nearly doubled over, as though she had been struck.

Her meddling had killed them. Unwittingly she had condemned Tuptim to death.

"But—but you are the King," she whispered.

"And to remain such I cannot undermine ability to command loyalty—which *I must have* to keep country secure!"

Anna looked up at him desperately. "You have the power to lead your people in any direction you wish! I have seen it!"

King Mongkut shook his head. "Now is not the

time to change ways things are done!"

Anna straightened. She gazed directly into his eyes and said, "From my own experience, I would have thought differently."

"Your own experience, Mem, should have given you deeper insight, so you not be so big a disappointment to me."

Anna flushed, looking—and feeling—as though she had been slapped. For a charged moment they stood facing each other in silence, her expression more potent than any words she might hurl at him. The King stared back at her unflinchingly, his granite will a shield for his convictions.

Then, at last, Anna shook her head. Without curtsying, she turned and strode back through the Great Hall. The King's gaze burned into her as she left.

twelve

The execution was scheduled for the next morning. A royal edict announced that a *parachik*—a corrupted monk—and a *nang ham* were to die at the fifth hour after sunrise. It was signed by the King.

An ox cart drew Tuptim and Balat through a jeering crowd, onlookers shouting abuse at them from the edge of the field where a tattered banner reading SIAMESE CRICKET CLUB dangled forgotten from a tree. Tuptim's arms cradled her lover's broken body. She caressed his bloodstained scalp, her eyes scanning the crowd for Anna Leonowens, but Anna was not there.

Guards cleared a path as the cart jounced along. It passed the carriages of Lady Jao Jom Manda Ung and her companions, who gazed out with self-satisfied expressions, nodding to each other. When the cart reached the center of the field it stopped. A broad platform stood there, the bamboo still damp and smelling freshly cut. On a smaller platform stood Justice Phya Phrom. As the guards dragged the prisoners, Tuptim raised her head and locked eyes with the magistrate.

"There is still time to confess, Lady Tuptim," he said, inclining his head to her. Behind him stood an executioner dressed in red, a long curved sword cradled in one arm, a handful of white blossoms in the other.

Tuptim's clear voice rang out above the crowd's din. "What is death compared to truth?"

The justice studied the trembling young woman— her dignity cloaking her fear, her pale face lifted to his. He said, "So be it."

He turned and read from the edict. "And for crimes against the state and the holy Buddha himself, Lady Khun Jao Tuptim and priest Khun Phra Balat are here and now to be put to death as a reminder to all that such actions will not be tolerated."

He nodded at the executioner and stepped down from the platform. The executioner followed, climbing the steps to the broader stand where Tuptim and Balat waited side by side. The guards moved forward, grabbing the prisoners and pushing them into a single stockade. The crowd roared as their hands and legs were bolted in place. Then the guards bowed and climbed down.

The executioner *waied* deeply before the two prisoners, begging their forgiveness. He stood, placed the white flowers in their hands, and turned away. Drums began to pound, thrumming louder and louder as the executioner swayed and lunged, performing a ritual dance as hypnotic as the drums' measured beat. In the field, a thousand eyes watched, bright with anticipation. Others, like Tuptim's servant Phim, prostrated themselves in awe at the young woman's devotion.

The drums beat faster, the executioner whirled and leaped. Balat murmured a prayer, then turned to Tuptim, his eyes brilliant with love. He smiled.

"*Pai sawan na,*" he whispered. *Go now to heaven, Tuptim*.

As she stared back at him, her eyes grew clear and unafraid. A look of great peace crept over her face. Her gaze remained one with Balat's, as around them the drums thundered and the sun glinted off

245

the twirling blade of the executioner's sword.

And then, suddenly, Balat's smile was no longer there. A shout rose, terrible in its frenzied joy, as white blossoms scattered across the bamboo platform.

But Tuptim remained unafraid. "*Pai sawan na, Balat,*" she whispered. Then she turned her head to stare serenely at the crowd and closed her eyes.

From Anna's house the drums sounded like muted thunder. When they abruptly grew silent, she was standing in a corner of her bedroom with her arms crossed tightly against her chest. Her breath came in hoarse gasps. In the unearthly stillness that descended, the house around her seemed to grow dark, speared with flashes of white and crimson.

She began to pace mindlessly. A terrible expression crept across her face, as though she were one of the spirit puppets repesenting a dreadful *phi* in a shadow play. Back and forth, back and forth. With each step her breathing grew louder and more ragged, her eyes so wide, they seemed to be staring into an abyss. On the hundredth pass across the room she found herself staring at her bookshelf, its titles seeming to waver in the air before her.

Vivarium Life

Oliver Twist

Uncle Tom's Cabin . . .

With a strangled cry her hand slashed at them. Books flew everywhere as she ripped them from the shelves, tearing the pages out and throwing them around the room in an animal rage. Glass shattered, wood splintered; the last volume tore through the window shutters and landed in the garden outside.

"*Mother!*"

Louis ran into the room, Moonshee and Beebe trying to restrain him but he was too strong. He halted short at the sight of his mother crouched on the floor amidst drifts of torn paper and binding, her hair wild, her breath coming in short bursts.

"Mother?"

She could not see him. Louis' eyes widened with fear. Beebe crept close to him, her arms enveloping the boy as he turned and hid his face in her skirts and began to cry. Silently, Moonshee and Bebe drew him away, closing the door behind them.

• • •

Late that night a small group of men stood in silence at the edge of the execution field. Where the bamboo platform had been, King Mongkut stood alone, gazing dully at the ground. The stocks were still there, waiting to be returned to the Court of Justice. The moon shone brightly overhead, and there was the sound of distant chanting.

"*Dek nak*," he whispered. *She was so young* . . .

He started back toward his waiting men. Something glistened in the moonlight, and he stopped. Stooping, he found a crushed bouquet of white orchids. He picked them up, turning them over in his hands, then set them atop the abandoned stocks and walked away.

The next day Louis Leonowens sat by himself on the pier in front of their house, whacking leechee nuts with his cricket bat. Inside, Moonshee removed the portrait of Queen Victoria from her place of honor on the wall. He shared a stricken look with his wife as he headed downstairs past Beebe and Anna, packing up the house in silence.

It was midday when the Kralahome looked up from his desk to see Mycroft Kincaid being escorted in.

The Englishman nodded at him, mopping his brow with a handkerchief as crimson as his face.

"I am absolutely baffled how you people survive this heat."

"Five minutes, Mr. Kincaid," the Kralahome said coldly. "I suggest you not waste them."

Undeterred, Kincaid stuck the handkerchief back in his pocket. "I don't suppose I could get a glass of water." At the Kralahome's icy stare he went on. "Right. Then I shall come straight to the point. I do a lot of business with the Siamese, many of whom have ended up dead in recent months. And I have discovered that this is all part of an elaborate hoax, to make you think we British are the villains.

"But I happen to know we're not. How I came about this little bit of information has cost me a small fortune, but—I think I'm about to become your best friend."

The Kralahome turned and barked at a servant. "Get this man something to drink!"

An hour later Kincaid had departed. The Kralahome was walking beside King Mongkut in the palace's grand concourse. On the walls hung a series of Western-style paintings by the King's intimate, Khrua In Khong, showing gathering armies and black clouds swelling above a storm-tossed sea.

". . . and so Alak's mercenaries will be dressed as palace guards."

The King stopped and stared bleakly at the wall. "A Trojan horse."

The Kralahome nodded. "Yes. Once he has taken the palace, he'll blame the coup on Burma and launch a full-scale attack using those troops of yours already protecting the border."

"He seeks to finish what Taksin only dreamed of."

"Taksin was insane."

"No. Taksin was betrayed. As we are now. As was my brother . . ."

The King walked off alone, and a long silence descended upon the concourse. After waiting in vain for him to speak, the distressed Kralahome said, "Your Majesty, he will not stop until all of your children are in velvet sacks."

"So much hate, so close to my heart." The King turned back to his Prime Minister. "How long before he reaches the city?"

"Kincaid thought a week, maybe less."

The Prime Minister watched helplessly as his King turned and strode down the corridor, Mongkut's eyes searching desperately for an answer within the canvases there. A man of peace, a man who had spent his life striving to find common ground between his own country and the encroaching West, a man whose sense of justice could be shaken but never compromised. He finally stopped, in front of a framed scroll bearing an inscription from the last century.

"And my armies?"

"They will never reach the palace in time."

"Then he has already won."

The King took a few more steps, then paused, gazing at the next mural—older still, a painting on silk depicting the joyous celebration surrounding the discovery of a sacred white elephant in the northern forest near Omkoi. Suddenly he turned.

"No." The Kralahome stared in astonishment as the King's face lit. "Recall the army. Send my fastest horses! Then announce to the people we have just received glad tidings."

The Kralahome shook his head. "Glad tidings, Your Majesty?"

"Yes!" cried the King. He gestured, laughing, at the ancient silken mural. "*See kao chang*—the sacred white elephant! A very good augury indeed . . ."

He hurried down the corridor to his study as the Kralahome stared after him in bewilderment.

Anna's caravan of carts and carriages, piled high with trunks and woven baskets and boxes, pots and pans and brass lamps, threaded its way to the harbor. A strangely jubilant crowd slowed their progress—lines of men and women playing cymbals and trumpets and tambourines, and the resonant music of the *ranad ek* and hundreds of bamboo pipes. When finally they reached the waterfront, Anna was exhausted. Holding Louis close, she stumbled from the carriage and headed for the annex where the *Newcastle's* purser was awaiting them as arranged. Behind them Moonshee and Beebe fought through the crowd, carrying as much of the household luggage as they could.

A frenzied, yet undeniably joyous, sort of bedlam prevailed along the entire harbor. Master and slave, old and young, wealthy merchants and penniless beggars, sang and cheered, and shouted raucously to the consternation of Anna and her family.

"I don't understand it." She frowned, shaking her head, then ran a hand across her sweltering brow. "It's too late in the season for another harvest festival . . ."

"Mother, doesn't *see kao chang* mean white ele-

252

phant?" Louis stood on tiptoe, trying to peer over the celebratory throng. "Do you think they *found* one?!"

"Yes!" A Siamese trader turned, beaming, from arranging his wares along a low bench. "White elephant in Prachin Buri! Entire village has seen it! The first in twenty years!"

Anna fumbled among her things until she found her purse, then placed Louis's hand firmly in Moonshee's. "Moonshee, watch him. I'll see to our tickets."

Louis looked as though he was about to cry. "I don't want to go, Mother. I don't want to leave my friends."

Moonshee gently stroked his head. "Your mother has much on her mind, little brother."

"The King has done *good* things, too!" Louis protested. "Even you—"

"Louis, why we are leaving is over ideas." Anna turned and spoke to him firmly. "The way people think. Who they are."

Louis shook his head. "You said the Siamese are people just like us. What about Chulalongkorn? Doesn't he matter anymore?"

Anna winced, hearing her own words thrown back at her. "Believe me, sweetheart," she said, struggling for an answer. "I know how difficult this is."

Turning, she began to fight her way through a long line of revelers. Abruptly the crowd parted around her. In the sudden space and relative quiet, Anna stood, catching her breath. A shadow fell across the ground at her feet. She looked up and found herself face to face with the Kralahome.

He was alone—the first time she had ever seen him without his retinue. Anna straightened and said, "You stopped me once before. It will not happen again."

She started to pass him and noticed that his hands were trembling.

"Sir." The Kralahome stared at her, his eyes brilliant. "You of all are most aware that there are certain boundaries Kralahome cannot cross. One being to contradict King."

"Yes, and God help him," Anna said angrily. "Now, if you'll excuse me . . ."

But the Kralahome just stood there. He looked around to make sure they were not being overheard, then lowered his voice and spoke with great difficulty.

"There is no white elephant, sir."

Anna gazed at him without understanding. The crowd jostled them as he went on. "King invented sighting so that he can escort royal family to greet imaginary beast, as is tradition."

He took a breath. Anna looked puzzled. "I don't understand."

"Sir, there is a traitor marching on the palace. Deception's only purpose is to hide royal children at monastery in Nong Khai. I have been deeply distrustful of you, but my King believes you are wise . . . "

His eyes welled. "Most probably, even should deception succeed, harm may be fatal. Please, Mem—you are only one who can persuade him to stay with children until army returns and palace is secure."

Merriment exploded all around them as Anna stood, silent. Finally she nodded, then turned. "Moonshee, Beebe—tell them to hold our things, please."

"Mother?" Louis ran to her side. "What is it? Is it—"

"A change of plans," Anna said, her voice expressionless. She looked at the Kralahome. "Please, lead us to him, Your Excellency."

Above the jetty outside the Grand Palace, a red banner with a white elephant fluttered in the breeze.

Hundreds of others flew from the palace's spires and ramparts, and from the upper deck of the royal steamer where it was berthed, being loaded for the expedition. Its prow was carven into the image of a huge garuda, eyes set with emerald green glass, its lacquered scales glistening gold and scarlet in the sun.

Thousands of well-wishers thronged the banks of the river, getting ready to send off the King and his entourage. The air rang with the sound of the court musicians, playing traditional instruments and brass horns, everyone united by their joy in the discovery of the sacred elephant.

Resplendent in a white uniform, King Mongkut emerged onto the palace quay. He was followed by his children, led by a remarkably mature-looking Prince Chulalongkorn. The boy wore his orange monk robes and his hair was beginning to grow in; he was flanked by bodyguards, as was his father. As the crowd's cheers grew deafening, the royal family walked slowly down the pier, ready to join the cortege gathering on the river.

"Everything in order, gentlemen?" the King asked his bodyguards.

"We have fireworks to announce sighting, musicians for the journey," Nikorn replied. "And gifts for the governor of Prachin Buri."

The King nodded. "Let us hope his spies are convinced."

Along the bank walked a file of royal astrologers, blessing the procession. As they did, a fantastic chain reaction occurred—wave after wave of Siamese prostrated themselves, honoring their king, until for as far as the eye could see there was a seemingly endless expanse of prone bodies. The King continued walking toward the royal steamer and then abruptly stopped.

Across the sea of worshipers, a small figure waited upon the dock.

Anna . . .

The King could not be certain if he had spoken her name aloud or not. For a long, awkward moment they stood, staring at each other above all those silent worshipers. Then, closing her eyes and drawing a deep breath, Anna curtsied. Quickly the King made his way toward her. His children waited obediently for the command to follow.

"Your Majesty. I have just been informed of the nature of your expedition."

The King stopped warily, spotting Louis and

Moonshee and Beebe standing to one side, and the Kralahome lying prostrate beside her.

"And," Anna continued, choosing her words with care, "I would like to ask you a few questions about the danger involved, as I have heard, at times, that wild elephants cannot be reasoned with."

The King's gaze flickered from Anna to his Prime Minister. "I am surprised Kralahome take time to arouse such curiosity, rather than make sure Mem not miss her boat."

He turned away, gesturing for all to rise. As the assembled multitude did so, he strode toward the gangway, passing Anna and the valiant Kralahome without another look.

"I have already missed it, Your Majesty." Her soft voice followed him. "So that I might speak with you."

The King stopped. He turned to her, eyes narrowing, then looked at the thousands waiting expectantly on the riverbanks; the astrologers and royal musicians, servants and nobles, concubines and royal wives; and last of all the long, patient line of the King's children.

"King cannot miss his boat," he said. Then, with a glance at the Prime Minister, he began to board the steamer.

Anna nodded, touched by his sense of duty. "Yes, I know." Something in her tone moved him to look back. "Which is why," she went on, "if it would not be inconvenient, we should like to go with you." She glanced at the delighted Louis, then turned to the King again.

The Kralahome stared at her in surprise. King Mongkut's expression changed to one of utter consternation. "Jungle is no place for proper English teacher, Mem."

The slightest hint of a smile played around her mouth. "No, Your Majesty, it is not. But the presence of one in your cortege might help ensure this display. Something I feel, for many reasons, I would very much like to do."

And, beckoning to Louis, Moonshee, and Beebe, Anna Leonowens marched onto the royal steamer. Overwhelmed, the King stared after her until finally his emotions overcame his reserve.

"You are a puzzlement," he said, and boarded.

It took almost an hour for the members of the royal family to settle themselves, taking their seats on long benches and cushioned chairs beneath brilliantly colored awnings made more vibrant with wreaths of orchids and jasmine, hibiscus and ginger

259

blossom. But at last the steamer was ready to depart. Its horn blew deafeningly; the onshore crowd cheered. With a fanfare of trumpets and horns, the boat pulled away from the jetty. An armada of smaller craft followed it, covered with flowers. King Mongkut stood high up on the canopied platform, gazing out upon the throng of joyful people—his people, his family all of them. They covered the landing and riverbank, and all the steps and terraces of the royal palace, banging drums and tambourines and waving rainbow-colored banners emblazoned with the sacred white elephant.

On the deck just below where the King stood, Louis perched on a high bench and blew his bugle in return, much to the delight of the court musicians, who echoed his fanfare.

"Now, now, little brother," scolded Moonshee. As Louis frowned in mock dismay, Moonshee confiscated the bugle and tucked it into the outside pocket of one of their bags.

Late in the afternoon, they reached the Langkawi inlet. Mountains rose violet and green against the sky as the royal steamer glided past, the garuda staring out proudly at the smooth, dark surface of the river and the limestone cliffs rising above them. Anna, too, stared into the water, though her expression was less sanguine than the garuda's. Across the deck, King Mongkut sat alone in a chair, watching her.

"When a woman who has much to say says nothing, her silence can be deafening." He smiled kindly, but Anna looked away. "I wish to thank you, Mem, for your courage."

Anna stared out at the limestone cliffs. "I thought I never wanted to see you again."

"I had a vision last night, of Tuptim and her priest," the King said softly. "I think by touching us all, they have fulfilled their destiny and achieved eternal peace." He hesitated, and added, "Through birth and rebirth, we Buddhists hope to learn from our mistakes."

He smiled, but his eyes were troubled, almost desolate. Anna stared at him and shook her head. "You said I had never accepted the loss of my husband."

"I had no right."

"It was true." With difficulty Anna mustered her own reassuring smile. "But now I realize it is not enough to merely survive. Life is far too precious. Especially when you are a Christian and only allowed one."

"Why did you come back?"

"Because I cannot imagine a Siam without you."

She held his look, and the King sudddenly felt powerless to hide his feelings toward her. He looked away, troubled, as she went on.

"Your Majesty, wouldn't your destiny be better fulfilled if you remained with your children in the safety of the monastery?"

"King does not hide from his enemies."

"Nor should he face this one without his armies."

"Alak believes I am bound for Prachin Buri. By the time he discovers I am not, I will be united with my armies to defend the palace."

His hand reached out to touch hers, ever so briefly, but it was enough. Anna nodded, and for a few minutes as they sat upon the deck there was no language that stood between them, no class or race or distance, only silence and the gentle motion of the steamer, and an understanding that extended far, far beyond words.

The limestone cliffs were riddled with caves, and it was in one of these that General Alak, the scar-faced leader of his forces, and their ranking officers met that night. The mercenaries wore the uniforms of the King's army and not of Burma. On the table before them was a large map of Bangkok. The general stabbed at it with a finger as a mercenary scout finished giving his report.

"The royal steamer has been abandoned near Lopburi. The King travels east on foot, away from Prachin Buri."

The scar-faced leader looked troubled. "If he is lying about the elephant, what other scheme has he concealed?"

As General Alak listened, his features tightened. "Are the children with him?"

The scout nodded. "Yes."

"Where would he take them?" demanded the leader.

General Alak walked to the entrance to the cavern. He stood there for several minutes, scanning the landscape outside and trying to determine the exact strategy his King had devised. At last he turned back to the others.

"There is a monastery in Non Khai. Mongkut spent half his life there."

"His sanctuary," muttered the scar-faced leader.

"Yes." Briskly, General Alak began rolling up his map. "The entire Chakri dynasty comes to us. We must not keep them waiting."

• • •

Louis stood in the moonlight, dejectedly feeding hay to one of the royal pack elephants. Beside him, Anna passed their luggage up to where Moonshee and Beebe stood, a trifle unsteadily, in the over-loaded *howdah*.

"But I want to see the white elephant," Louis said for the hundredth time.

"It's just a myth, Louis." Anna reached for the last trunk, groaning. "I'm sorry."

"But *why* do we have to go to the monastery?"

Anna lay a hand on his arm. "Come now, Louis. It's time to go."

A short distance away, the King knelt before the ruins of a giant stone Buddha, its monolithic form rising like gray smoke from the forest greenery. Around him were his children, prone as their father was as they all prayed for guidance. Anna glanced over at them, torn between heartbreak and anger. Her expression changed when she saw the figure of Nikorn, the King's bodyguard, suddenly emerge from the jungle. Ignoring protocol, he strode through the little crowd of prostrate bodies and up to the King. As he did so, the children raised their heads, wondering who dared interrupt their father at his prayers—and why?

Nikorn bent beside the King, whispering to him and gesturing. Anna turned to see what he was pointing at—the other two bodyguards, Noi and Pitak, peering through a telescope perched on the bluff overlooking the valley. Without a word the King sprang to his feet and hurriedly joined his guards. Anna followed him, watching as Pitak stepped away from the lens and the King moved behind his instrument. He stared into it, refocusing, then straightened. His face had gone ashen.

"What is it?" Anna whispered.

Mongkut gestured at the telescope. She bent to look through, and saw creeping into the valley from the hills a thousand jolts of flame, moving steadily and relentlessly as lava down the hillside: General Alak's legion of mercenaries.

"They will reach the bridge by dawn," Noi said expressionlessly. "We cannot outrun them, Your Majesty."

Pitak shook his head. "And there is still no sign of our troops, Your Majesty."

"Do not let them see your fear, gentlemen," replied the King. He began giving instructions to the three men, who quickly turned and shouted to the palace guards and slaves to break camp.

"What has happened?" cried Anna.

"You and the children must go on to Nong Khai without me. I will meet you there."

"No! I can see it in your eyes—something horrible is happening."

"Was not to be this way, Mem." The King gazed dully at the telescope. "Alak's army has found us. If he crosses the bridge, everyone I love will die."

Anna blanched. "But they're just children . . ."

"Yes, and each one heir to the Chakri throne. Now you must hurry."

Anna glanced at the bodyguards surrounding the armory wagon, gathering flintlock rifles and coils of rope and twine. Other men began quickly and soundlessly to remove dozens of barrels from wagons and discarded *howdahs*. One barrel jostled another, and a thin stream of black powder sifted out as the spools of wire were handed around to grim-faced men.

"What are you going to do?" she whispered.

"Blow up the bridge."

"Will that stop him?"

"It will if he's on it."

Anna blinked, trying to keep tears from coming. "Promise me—promise me I will see you again."

Slowly he raised his hand to her face and, as

though she were one of his sleeping children, stroked her cheek with his fingertips. Anna moved toward him, until her mouth brushed against his palm.

Behind them there was a crash of leaves and underbrush: the King's bodyguards had returned. Anna dipped her head, turning from the King's gaze as Prince Chulalongkorn, the royal children, and their mothers surrounded them. Nearby stretched a line of wagons and elephants, awaiting their departure.

"But, Father!" For a moment Prince Chulalongkorn looked neither mature nor monkish, only extremely disappointed. "Never, *ever* has such an expedition excluded the children of the palace!"

King Mongkut looked down at him. He smiled sadly and said, "My son, there are many things you will come to understand when you are older."

"Why can't I stay with you?"

"Because I need you to lead these people to the monastery."

Prince Chulalongkorn glared at him defiantly. And then, seeing something in his father's face he had never glimpsed before, defiance melted into confusion. "Father . . ."

The boy's voice fell to a whisper. "There isn't any white elephant, is there?"

King Mongkut took his son in his arms and cradled him, his cheek pressed against the boy's as he murmured in his ear.

"No, my brave heart. There is not." Eyes filling, the King gazed at his eldest son. "Take care of your brothers and sisters."

Chulalongkorn stared at him, devastated. Then, as the realization of his new responsibilities overcame him, he hugged him back.

"Yes, Your Majesty."

King Mongkut smiled. "I have never been more proud of you, my son." He turned, praying that the children would see only his smile and not the heartbreak behind it, as he wondered if he would ever see them again.

"Good. Now . . ." He opened his arms. "Come, come, come . . ."

They swarmed over him, laughing as they clung to his arms and legs, clambering onto him as though he were a mountain, a temple—a refuge.

And for a very little while, he was.

After the children departed, the King walked to where Nikorn and Pitak and Noi stood beside an oil lamp. When he reached them, he slid a hand into the pocket of his uniform jacket and withdrew three straws.

"The greatest honor goes to the shortest straw," he said.

Pitak drew first—a long straw. Then Noi—another. And finally Nikorn. His brave expression collapsed as he gazed at the finger-length of straw in his hand. "Let us hope it does not come to that," the King said gently.

As the caravan made its way through the forest, even the elephants seemed dispirited as they swayed slowly along the path. The failing sun sent shadows leaping among the trees, and everywhere Anna looked she imagined only gruesome things.

I can see how the phi *live here*, she thought grimly. Then, fighting despair, she glanced at Louis's elephant, lumbering alongside her own. The boy was asleep—Beebe had whispered that news down to Anna as soon as she appeared—but an insistent, rhythmic sound kept interrupting her thoughts. Anna stared up, frowning, until she sighted Louis's bugle, hanging from its lanyard and knocking against the side of the *howdah*. She looked at the bugle absently, her thoughts drifting to her son and

King Mongkut as her elephant bore her on slowly through the night.

The bridge at Nong Khai was serene and still when the King, Pitak, and Noi reached it at dawn. They had sent Nikorn on ahead, to do his work beneath its span, the King's final order like a falling axe:

"No matter what happens, blow this bridge."

Now mist shrouded the bridge's massive teak beams, the river flowing beneath in a slow chocolate-colored stream. Then the sun broke over the mountains, quartz pink, butter yellow, and a single white heron rose over the river like an omen. For an instant the King and his tiny retinue were silhouetted like the bird against the glowing sky. Then the King gave the stallion its head, and the great horse raced at full gallop down the mountainside, Pitak's and Noi's mounts close behind.

In a quarter-hour they reached the valley floor. They slowed, reining in their mounts as the horses reared skittishly at the sight of the bridge looming above them. King Mongkut dismounted, his eyes scanning the opposite bank as he walked his horse to the end of the span.

And there they were—the bridge pylons tightly

wrapped with barrels of black powder, wires leading from them and disappearing under the rank high grass. The King turned, shading his eyes as he gazed downriver. He could not see Nikorn, but he knew his bodyguard was there, hidden in the reeds with a clear view of the bridge, the detonator locked in his hand.

But he could not see Louis, high up on another bluff looking down into the valley. The boy had found the King's telescope among the caravan's supplies, and set it up at the edge of the cliff. "Mother, look!"

Anna turned from where she was repacking their things, Louis's bugle in her hand. "What is it?"

"The king is riding toward the bridge! See?"

"What?"

In her shock she dropped the bugle, then found herself staring down at it, the brass shining brightly in the mud like a spark, or a sword.

"Wait," she whispered, and slowly retrieved the instrument. "Just wait . . ."

In the valley below them, King Mongkut took a deep breath. For the moment he was at peace, knowing he had done all that he could to protect his people.

Then the breeze shifted. As it did, a faint rumbling could be heard. Moments later the ground beneath the King began to shake. The King and his bodyguards turned, staring at a sloping hill that rose above the opposite shore of the river. The rumbling grew louder, then louder still, until at last a figure appeared at the crest of the hill, outlined against the morning sky.

General Alak. He rode to the edge of the bridge, astride a black stallion more heavily built than the King's own, wearing black and crimson robes that snapped like a pennon in the breeze. Even from where he stood, the King could see the glint of sunlight from the barrel of a pistol slung at his waist, and the shining blade of the curved *kris* in his belt. There was a second man on horseback beside the general, the lean, scar-faced leader of the mercenaries, and behind him gathered an army of five hundred heavily armed warriors, on foot and horseback.

King Mongkut watched them impassively. The general's reaction was less composed. He raised his hand to slow the progress of his troops, and stared bewildered at the three men across the river. He and the scar-faced leader exchanged looks. King Mongkut simply waited.

"As the sun rises, it also sets," General Alak cried out at last. But there was a wary edge to his voice as he reined in his impatient horse, trying to keep it from racing across the bridge. "You are either incredibly brave or incredibly stupid."

Behind the King, Noi and Pitak glanced at each other, thinking the same thing.

"You saved my life once," the King shouted in reply. "And now I offer yours in return." He gestured at the waiting army. "Throw down your weapons, or you and your men will be slaughtered without mercy."

General Alak stared incredulously at the three small figures across the river. "I hardly think women and children with parasols are up to the task."

His men laughed, but their amusement died as King Mongkut led his bodyguards onto the bridge. When they reached the middle, they stopped.

General Alak turned to his henchman. "He's crazy," the scar-faced man sneered.

The general nodded. "He's bluffing."

And with that, Alak spurred his horse onto the bridge. Behind him his mercenaries hesitated, then fell in behind him, marching to where the King waited.

Flanking their monarch, Pitak and Noi rested their hands on their weapons. The King and his general regarded each other. There was more sadness and regret in that gaze than hostility: Alak's betrayal weighed heavily upon them both.

"Chowfa loved you like a brother," the King said in a low voice.

"It is your politics that killed him."

"As yours will kill you."

Slowly the King withdrew a cheroot from his pocket. The scar-faced leader's eyes flickered from side to side, searching for an unseen enemy force.

"That would be quite a feat," said General Alak, "since your armies are marching on Burma."

"My army is defending a peace that a man like you could never understand."

But General Alak was unswayed. "Your army is in the north."

The King nodded. "Yes."

And with that, His Gracious Majesty Somdetch P'hra Paramendr Maha Mongkut, King Rama IV, flicked a match. The incandescent spark glowed bluish-white in the morning haze, then died as he lit his cheroot.

"Defiant to the last," sneered the general. "As

each day the sun sets, so does the Chakri dynasty."

Downstream, Nikorn saw the match's flare, and knew it for the signal the King had commanded him to obey. Yet even as his shaking hand yanked at the cords, they did not move. Frantically he searched the trip lines, and saw that they were wedged under a rock.

No! He pulled desperately: They had only this chance, this moment. . . .

In the middle of the bridge, the King and his two bodyguards braced themselves for their deaths. Noi drew a long breath, and heard its echo as Pitak and King Mongkut did the same.

O Gracious Buddha, Thou Excellence of Perfection, I take refuge in thee; the King prayed, silently and in utter calm. *Thou who art called the Enlightened One, I take refuge in thee* . . .

Yet, witnessing their silence, General Alak saw not defeat and surrender, but a confident monarch's display of enormous power. He glanced around uneasily, wondering if Mongkut could possibly have an army behind him.

Surely not! And yet Mongkut's serenity, his conviction!

Where he sat hidden by the reeds, the distraught Nikorn finally gripped the detonator's plunger. He drew a last shuddering breath, offered a prayer begging forgiveness for killing his lord, and began to press it down—

—when suddenly a brilliant flash of light erupted on the hillside behind the King. Nikorn's hand fell into the water and he stared in astonishment, as a dozen rockets flared and exploded on the King's side of the river. King Mongkut steadied his horse, trying to conceal his amazement. His bodyguards did the same, and General Alak stared open-mouthed.

From the hillside echoed the triumphant strains of the British call to battle, joined by first one bugle and then another across the hills. Nikorn stared at the detonator in his hands, then at the bridge. More rockets exploded as the scar-faced leader and his troops tried the control their spooked mounts.

"He's brought the English?" the scar-faced man shouted, dumbfounded.

Behind him the orderly troops disintegrated. Horses reared and squealed, men cursed at each other as panic overtook the mercenaries.

"There is nobody!" General Alak shouted above the melee. "It's a trick!"

Enraged, he turned back to Mongkut. Fearing the

276

worst, Nikorn and Pitak inched closer to their King. More rockets exploded overhead, more bugles called for fire, as the King struggled to control his mount. His gaze remained locked on his betrayer as he stood his ground, determined to play his hand out to the death.

"Do not retreat! *It is a trick!*"

With a cry, General Alak yanked his pistol from his belt and aimed it at the King. In that instant a volley of fire came from Pitak and Noi. The general's mount screamed in terror, twisting so that it collapsed against King Mongkut's stallion. Both horses fell to the bridge, unseating their riders. Alak's horse bolted for freedom; Noi grabbed the King's stallion, calming it until Mongkut could mount him once more.

"*No!*" General Alak cried at his troops. But the sight of their fallen leader was too much for the mercenaries.

"We fight battles we can win!" yelled their scar-faced leader. He spun his mount, signaled retreat, and galloped back over the ridge. Soldiers scattered in all directions. General Alak stumbled to his feet and stood, alone, shouting at his fleeing troops.

"*There is no one!*"

As if in agreement with him, one by one the horns grew silent. The rockets stopped, and the last trailers of smoke floated off on the morning breeze. In the reeds, Nikorn carefully set down the detonator. King Mongkut tugged his stallion's reins, guiding him so that he could gaze down at the man who would have been king.

"Let me kill him," said Pitak, but the King shook his head.

"There are many ways to die," Mongkut said quietly. He spurred his horse and, followed by his bodyguards, started back across the bridge. "I want him to live with his humiliation."

The general watched him go, then turned to see the body of the scar-faced leader on the far bank, a long rifle slung across his body.

"This was not exactly the plan, Your Majesty," said Noi as they escorted the King off the bridge. The bodyguard's eyes remained fixed on the general.

"No," Mongkut replied. He glanced sideways, first at Noi, then Pitak. "You would have preferred mine?"

The three men smiled, feeling a sudden surge of joy at being alive. Their horses stepped from the bridge. Behind them, General Alak yanked the rifle from the dead man and lifted it to his shoulder. He took aim, leveling it at the King. Downriver, Nikorn opened his eyes from a thankful prayer and gazed in horror at the bridge.

"No!" he shouted. He scrambled madly for the detonator, grabbing it and depressing the plunger just as the general's finger tightened on the trigger.

With an ear-splitting roar, a massive fireball consumed the bridge. The King and his bodyguards were thrown from their mounts as the blast echoed through the valley, sending debris flying. The entire bridge bucked and snapped like a maddened serpent. Then with a sound like a thunderclap it collapsed into the river, burying General Alak and his dreams of glory.

The King found his makeshift defending army at the top of the ridge, safely hidden behind a thicket of bamboo. A busy troop of wives and concubines and children were lugging empty boxes of fireworks back to the *howdahs* and wagons. As he rode up, each and every one of them turned and *wai*ed proudly, hands and faces streaked with soot. The King nodded, continuing until he saw Louis, bugle slung around his neck as he helped the female court musicians pack away their instruments—and Anna Leonowens, her back to him as she bent over a carton.

"*You!*" the King cried.

Anna turned, startled. King Mongkut stared down, his expression unreadable, then dismounted and strode over to her.

"Why did you not go to monastery like King order!?"

Face smudged, hair completely disheveled, Anna rose to her full height and shouted back at him.

"Because I lost one man to the jungle, Your Majesty!" She blew away a loose strand and motioned to the crowd gathering around them. "And I was not about to let that happen again."

She whirled, pointing. Led by Prince Chula-longkorn, the entire royal family surged forward to surround their King—and father, husband, and lover—a bit tentatively, in light of his reaction to their disobedience. Clearing his throat, the Crown Prince stepped forward and bowed.

"Mem Anna not fully to blame, Father," he said. "After all, you did put me in charge."

For a long, long moment, the King was utterly speechless. Then, shaking his head, he turned to Louis and beckoned for his bugle. Proudly the boy handed it up to him. And the King smiled, remembering a bit of dinner-party conversation.

"'To sound English bugles in own defense . . .'"

Anna smiled. "Yes."

King Mongkut continued to stare thoughtfully at Louis's instrument. Finally he said, "When King say handful of men could save all Siam, he was most unusually correct."

He bowed slightly to Anna. For once she did not know what to say, but only gazed back at him, flustered. Then, without warning, a low murmur ran through the crowd around them, growing louder with each passing second. With a cry some of the women fell to their knees, while others looked around wonderingly.

"*Look!*" shouted Louis. All turned to see what he was pointing at.

At the top of the nearest ridge, something was moving—something huge. As the morning fog lifted, a herd of elephants emerged from the mist, making their way down to where a small stream flowed through the valley. As they drew nearer, cries of exultation rose from the watching Siamese. Everyone spotted the smaller creature walking with careful steps beside its elders—

A baby white elephant, its pale skin luminescent in the morning light.

"Siam is blessed . . . we are truly blessed . . ."

Hushed voices began whispering and uttering cries of thanks. Anna joined the rest in gazing transfixed at the enchanted herd as the elephants slowly crossed the stream, the valley brightening around them. Then, as if by magic, they once more disappeared into the trees. Anna blinked, feeling tears coming at last, and when the King turned to her again, he saw her staring at him, her blue eyes shining but her smile tinged with a great and ineffable sorrow.

thirteen

"... and with all reflecting on how close kindom come to ceasing to be ..."

Prince Chulalongkorn's voice cut through the clear night air, reciting the English words with precision. Before him on the Grand Terrace, his father sat at the head of the table, surrounded by the Kralahome and the entire royal family, along with scores of friends. A makeshift stage had been raised there, complete with a cardboard jungle behind which Anna prompted the actors, royal children in the costumes of classical dancers. One wore a mask meant to represent King Mongkut, another a mask with Anna's face carefully painted on it. The other children formed the cortege, while Prince Chulalongkorn narrated and the female court musicians accompanied him.

". . . most radiant dawn broke forth over tallest mountain, and it be then that all ears hear what all eyes suddenly see . . ."

He paused dramatically, then cried, "Great White Beast in infinite splendor!"

Nothing happened. Prince Chulalongkorn turned, frowning, and looked at Anna hiding in the wings. She waved her hand frantically, prompting him to repeat his line. Obediently he turned back to the audience.

"Great White Beast—"

And suddenly a papier-mâche elephant tore through the painted backdrop. Anna clapped her hand to her forehead and winced. King Mongkut and the diners smiled.

The Prince rattled on. "—and, as people rejoice with overwhelming joy—"

With a chorus of shrieks and giggles, the sacred white elephant swayed back and forth, then collapsed in a heap. The set tumbled down on top of it as the Prince continued valiantly, "And so most excellent conclusion to expedition echoed in every corner of Siam!"

"The end!" Louis's muffled voice rose from within the fallen pachyderm. The makeshift curtains closed. King Mongkut and the guests tried their best not to laugh; then the King stood, applauding, as the others joined in. All the children rushed around Anna, Louis struggling to pull the elephant's papier-mâche head from his own.

"Mem," said Prince Chulalongkorn, upset by the debacle. "This is play to commemorate monumental occasion. And we make fools of ourselves because of insufficent practice!"

The other children chimed in. Anna tried to calm them.

"I understand, truly, but the celebration was tonight, and we were duty bound to join it, were we not?"

Reluctantly her cast nodded. "Good," said Anna, smiling. "Now, I want you all to imagine *next* year, after you've had time to perfect things."

She looked up and caught King Mongkut still applauding. His gaze was not on the children but on her, staring at her the way he had on the mountaintop months ago. For an instant she was unable to look away. Then, turning back to her charges, she said, "Your—your father will be even more proud of you than he already is."

"And you, Mem?" asked Prince Chulalongkorn. "Will you be?"

She looked down into her prize pupil's shining eyes, and at the others around him, all of them staring at her with utter love and devotion. Her children: Siam's next generation.

"I shall always be proud of you, my children. Always . . ."

Then, ducking her head so that they could not see her tears, she fled from the terrace.

The King found her a short time later, sitting in a dimly lit corner. Her handkerchief was in her hand, and her face was red and streaked with tears. From the terrace faint music played, and he could look down and see his guests—including the children—waltzing joyously.

But here another music sounded: the faint strains of Mozart, rising from a wooden music box set on a small table beside Anna. As he approached her, she looked up, vainly trying to dry her eyes. She coughed, then gestured at the music box.

"I—I ordered this for the children some time ago. A fine example of—of scientific thinking, because—because music is mathematical in nature, and . . ."

The King stooped beside her, took the handkerchief, and dabbed a tear from her cheek. His own eyes were deeply sorrowful. "Chords constructed from notes in intervals of thirds, and so on . . ."

"Precisely," sniffed Anna.

They stared at one another. At last Anna said, thickly, "I would just like to know why, if science can explain the mystery of something as beautiful as music—why it is unable to posit a solution for a King and a schoolteacher."

The King smiled sadly. "The manner in which people might understand such new possibilities is, I am afraid, also process of evolution."

Anna nodded. "Everything in Siam has its own time . . ."

"Even if King is also wanting it to be different."

She looked away. "I—I must still go, Your Majesty. As a very dear friend once said, 'My path is as it should be.'"

"This I, too, realize."

She took a breath, nodded, and tried to smile. King Mongkut smiled back, then asked, "Where will you be going?"

She hesitated. "England."

"Home." He nodded. "This is good, Mem. Very good for Louis as well."

She took another breath. "Yes. And one day, when

you come visit your new trading partners, you must drop by so we may finally take tea together."

The King continued to stare at her, searching her face.

"What?" asked Anna.

"I am wondering if, given circumstances, it is appropriate for King to ask . . ."

He paused. ". . . Anna to dance."

Struggling to control herself, she replied, "I have danced with a king before, Your Majesty."

"And I, an Englishwoman."

Slowly he held out his hand. Anna placed hers in his, and he guided her down toward the Grand Terrace, his other hand circling her waist.

For a long moment, with the moonlight streaking the air and the faint sweet strains of Mozart continuing to echo around them, Anna and the King of Siam stared into one another's eyes, knowing this last moment would be theirs, always, sending its own echo down through the rest of their lives.

"Until now, Madam Leonowens," the King whispered, "I did not understand supposition man could be satisfied with only one woman."

Anna bit her lip. Then, smiling through her tears, she nodded as the King led her out onto the terrace, where they joined their family and friends in the waltz.

And all who saw them then—the Kralahome, the King's wives and lovers and children, Anna's son, Louis, but most of all Crown Prince Chulalongkorn—all who gazed upon them that night knew they gazed upon the most enduring true nobility, of heart as well as spirit.

fourteen

It is always surprising how small a part of life is taken up by meaningful moments. Most often they are over before they start, even though they cast a light on the future, and make the person who originated them unforgettable.

Anna had shined such a light on Siam. And even after I ascended to my father's place upon the throne, I never, ever forgot her.

fifteen

Forty years passed before the King came to tea. When he did arrive, it was not His Gracious Majesty King Mongkut, Rama IV, who knocked at the door of Anna Leonowens's modest cottage in the English countryside, but his son Chulalongkorn, King Rama V. As the motorcade of Daimlers pulled into the drive, Anna nervously smoothed her white hair, checking the table for the last time. On the stove the kettle boiled; on the lacy tablecloth was set her best blue and white china and silver. She had already pulled the scones from the oven, spooned strawberry jam into a small bowl, and taken the clotted cream from the icebox. And she had even found her old tea cosy, the one she had put away for safekeeping years before, the one printed with a white elephant.

She wound the gramophone and put on a piece by Mozart—another favorite, her heart aching as the sweet, familiar strains filled the little room. When the knock came at the door, she bowed her head and took a deep breath. Then, smiling, her heart bursting with joy and expectation, she went to greet King Mongkut's eldest son.

They ate, and laughed, and wept, surrounded by souvenirs of Anna's travels and photographs of Louis and his children. Chulalongkorn's entourage waited outside in their cars, as the fire crackled merrily in the hearth and the shadows lengthened, and still they talked, the young student grown to a man and monarch, his teacher now a silver-haired but still beautiful grandmother.

"Never did I imagine, thirty years ago, that you would be here sharing tea with me, Your Majesty."

King Chulalongkorn regarded her fondly. "As I told my wife and children, when you were my teacher, you assured me all roads led to London."

Anna smiled and handed him a cup. "The world has changed so much since then, Your Majesty, in so many ways. Telephones, automobiles—and what would your father have said about men trying to build machines that can fly?"

"That it was his idea."

They laughed, and the King continued to gaze at her. "It is unfortunate he died so soon, and never had the chance to make this trip himself. He always hoped to."

Anna nodded and glanced aside, staring into the fire.

"Mem," King Chulalongkorn went on. "The reason I came to see you . . ."

She looked at him, puzzled, as he pulled a red silk pouch from his jacket pocket and placed it on the table in front of her.

"The day before my father died, he told me he wanted you to have this. But it wasn't until just recently that we finally located it, lodged somewhere in the back of an old desk."

Anna eyed the pouch tentatively as King Chulalongkorn urged her, "Please, Mem, he would be disappointed if you did not accept."

She glanced up and held his look, then hesitantly took the pouch and slowly opened it. When she saw what it held, she cried out.

"*Ooooh* . . ."

It was the ring bearing the symbol of the Sun and the Moon. Eyes filled with tears, Anna stared at it, unable to speak. Finally she took a deep breath and said, "I have always tried to impress upon my students how important it is to never lose one's composure . . ."

Her finger traced the image of the sun, as Mozart played on behind them. "I—I truly do not know what to say, Your Majesty—except that I am honored."

Then slowly, tenderly, she slid the ring onto the third finger of her left hand. After a moment she looked up. "I have something for you as well."

She reached beneath the table, withdrew a small wrapped package, and handed it to the King. He unwrapped it, his eyes filling. Nestled in a cardboard box was the dented bugle that had once saved his father's life.

"I shall treasure it always."

Anna nodded. "As I do its memory."

The King reached out warmly and took her hands. "It would bring me much pleasure, Mem Anna, if you would join me this evening for dinner in celebration of all that is wonderful about life."

Anna smiled. "I should like that, Your Majesty. I should like that very much."

• • •

Thanks to the vision of his father, King Mongkut, and the teachings of Anna Leonowens, King Chulalongkorn not only maintained Siam's independence, but also abolished slavery, instituted religious freedom, and reformed the judicial system, transforming Siam from a feudal society to a country that was truly free and prepared to enter the twentieth century.